WHAT BECOMES
OF A BROKEN SOUL

WHAT BECOMES
OF A BROKEN SOUL

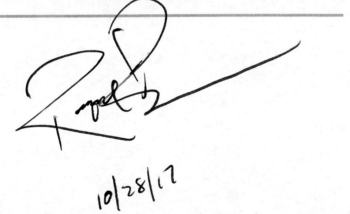

10/28/17

Raquel M. R. Thomas

ISBN: 1545218595
ISBN-13: 9781545218594
Library of Congress Control Number: 2017905555
CreateSpace Independent Publishing Platform
North Charleston, South Carolina

A DEDICATION TO YOU

This book is dedicated to my lifelines, Roman and Raquel, my children. Thank you for giving me an unknown strength beyond the natural strength that runs through me. You are the very best parts of me, and I cannot imagine this life without you. You both are gifts from God, and your lives give me a reason every day to keep pushing. Providing a great path for you is now my legacy; I am building this legacy for you. You are my absolute world, and God blessed me beyond measures when he gave you both to me. Mommy loves you.

This book is also dedicated to Gina Cooper, who told me in 2010, "You should write a book, because your story inspires me every day." Gina, because of you, I started pursuing my first childhood fantasy of becoming an author. Thank you for always believing in me and encouraging me. When I had nothing, you filled many empty spaces in my life. You loved me as if I were your child, and that saved my life. You taught me the small things that mattered when I entered the big world of corporate America and business ownership. Thank you. I love you.

To every supporter from South Carolina, thank you for following my journey. Your support gave me a little more fight every day to live my dreams out loud. As a little girl, I started dreaming of a life of greatness, and it was there in my room I knew that I wanted to become a dream catcher! This is for every child who can't see past their today: know that there is hope, and anything is possible. I am living proof.

CONTENTS

ACKNOWLEDGMENTS

As I sit here and listen to "You Gotta Believe" from the *My Life* album by Mary J. Blige (one of her best albums and one of the best R&B albums of all time), I want to be sure to acknowledge everyone who played a part in my overall success. So if I forget anyone, please know that it isn't my heart that should be charged but my brain.

To start, I will say thank you to my parents, Audrey and Walter Mitchell. Without you, I wouldn't be here to carry out my dreams. Thank you for giving me life and bringing me into this world. Also, to my granny who has passed on to a great life with God, thank you for letting me know I was born to succeed and was going to do something with my life beyond the drugs and alcohol that attacked everything around us. To my godmother, Catherine Sims, thank you for praying over my life and for always covering me in prayer.

You are the best godmother a kid could ever ask for. It is because of you I take *my* godparent role seriously. Thank you for being a great example.

HSJ, thank you for twenty-plus years of a little bit of everything! Thank you for the great seasons and memories we shared. Thank you for always listening to me live my dreams out loud. TAY.

To my blood family—aunts, uncles, and cousins—thank you for the great moments we have shared throughout my life, although few and far between; thank you for the memories.

To my sisters and brothers from other mothers (you all know who you are), thank you for your support and encouragement throughout the process of achieving my goals. Thank you for showing up to give me a familiar face in the crowd. Most important, thank you for being my family and never leaving me alone.

To my godchildren and their mothers and fathers, thank you for being special parts of my life. Thank you for loving me and preparing me for motherhood. You all are very special to me, and I'm blessed to have been given the opportunity to be your godmother.

To all my coaches and teachers in high school and college, thank you for seeing something special within me beyond my athletic skill. Thank you for helping me become a better person.

To my DMR family, thank you for believing in the brand and always being willing to go the extra mile. To my business partners—wow! Your trust in allowing me to navigate is second to none. Thank you for always being right behind me, no matter what.

Tre Tailor, I can't say thank you enough for believing in me and being a major part of the movement I am creating. Thank you for always knowing what to say to me when I'm searching for greater meaning and understanding. Thank you for covering me.

To RDT, thank you for taking this ride with me. Thank you for being my sounding board and always listening when I need an ear. Most important, thank you for always being my friend.

Last, thank you to all my supporters and my social-media family. In this day and age, social media is probably the largest platform we all have. Everyone has a choice of whom to follow and friend, and I thank you for allowing me to be a part of your platform. I thank you for listening to my voice through social media. Thank you for your kind words, prayers, and encouragement.

Raquel RT3

PROLOGUE

Today marks one year from the day my life changed forever. It started with a call. Richard had taken many cruises, and along the way, he gained points as a reward. The points would discount the price of the cruise, but Richard couldn't use the points toward his cruise payment because his cruise had been paid for by a third party. Tim and Mona thought this would be an incentive for me to say yes to going on the cruise—a cruise that Tim and Mona, my very best friends since Howard University where we first met, pushed me to join. This call started the communication between Richard and me. Our conversation was brief, though we discussed applying the reward points to my payment for the cruise. Richard had earned reward points that were expiring; he knew he wouldn't be able to use the points, so he wanted to give them away.

The cruise line had designed this trip for young people to get away and enjoy a carefree, five-day adventure—and I certainly had fun! During my time on the *Royal Fantasy*, I met new people and was a part of something very different from my everyday life. The trip had attracted people from all walks of life, including those lost in the play world. The play world was a world where everything was fantasy, with no real responsibility. In the play world, the only job was to have fun! There to free myself from my own unhappiness, I fell into the middle of all this. Needless to say, this cruise was the beginning of a new life for me—a life of freedom and a newfound love. The cruise was filled with drinking, partying, and all the things that happen when drinking and partying mix. I celebrated by spending time with my friends who had convinced me to come on this cruise. I met many new people and exchanged numbers with most of them. In most cases, I didn't keep the numbers I received, but I wanted to be polite regardless of my intentions.

When I returned from the cruise, my heart was free, and I walked away from a five-year relationship that no longer gave me what I needed. I walked into being a single woman again. Living only for myself was my new focus, and I was ready to provide for myself and myself only. My new goal in life was to be happy, and I found that happiness in being single and in living freely, seeing the world with new eyes.

I received a message on Facebook from Richard, inviting me to his annual dinner party. Who would have thought I would ever speak to him again? Oddly enough, I had been invited to this very dinner by Mona as her guest, and I'd accepted, so I guess fate had secured my presence at this dinner. I told Richard I would be there to celebrate. My thoughts started to wander as I wondered how uncommon it was to receive an invitation to a dinner twice and not have a friendship with the man hosting it. However, Richard had assisted me with booking the cruise, and I did spend time with him on the cruise. So I guess it wasn't that uncommon. This would be the first time we'd seen each other since the cruise.

I arrived at the dinner party alone and on time, as I lived only minutes away, and Mona was running late. I had stopped to pick up a card, because I didn't want to go empty-handed, but it's difficult to purchase something for someone you don't know very well. I had only spent a few days with Richard on the cruise; prior to the cruise, I knew nothing about him. Although I don't remember what the card said, I do know it was a nice and simple message. Richard greeted me at the door. It was a pleasant surprise, as his smile was inviting, and his hug was refreshing. There were only a few people there when I arrived, including Dana, Richard's ex-girlfriend, with whom he still lived. They had remained roommates because they couldn't break their rental lease. They were an odd couple indeed, and from the outside looking in, she appeared to be the help or a good friend preparing the food for Richard's guests. I never would have assumed they had been a couple at one time. It was a good thing I already knew her name, as our introduction was perfunctory at best. I introduced myself to Dana, and her response was barely a response.

She said, "Oh, hi. Richard mentioned you from the cruise." She said this with a slight grin on her face and walked away. Dana was tall with long hair. While I didn't find her attractive, I could see how one would be attracted to her.

The dinner was great. I've always been a very modest woman, but I also know my strengths when in a room full of people. I stand five foot five with a Coke-bottle figure and a smile that can dazzle. I had just cut my hair, and it came to my shoulders; it was full of body and a healthy shine. I considered my hair to be 90 percent of my sexy. My appearance catches most eyes, and my intellect often takes a room by storm. The dinner was filled with those who were drawn to my inviting smile. After eating, I played cards and laughed with many of the guests. By the time Mona arrived, I had already become friendly with the others at the party, including Richard—I've always had a God-given talent for pulling people in and making them feel comfortable. Although I took in a lot from the other guests, I gave very little of myself in return. I shared very little about myself in my conversations that night. By the time Mona arrived, I was very happy to see my friend's smiling face. She and I continued to float around the room, sharing smiles with everyone.

Richard joined us shortly after Mona's arrival. He wanted to know whether I planned to go on the cruise the next year. My initial answer was no, but he and Mona eventually wore me down. Finally, I said yes. Before I knew it, hours had passed, and Mona had to leave to fulfill other duties that night. Mona was a bartender at a local club, and she needed to be on time for her work shift. Earlier that evening, she had mentioned the connection she'd noticed between Richard and me, and I'd found her comment odd, considering I had not had a real conversation with him outside of the small talk typical of a dinner gathering.

In fact, I'd spent more time talking to Malcolm, a friend of Richard's, who had traveled from out of state to attend the dinner. He was a very nice married man who was successful in his career, and his smile was inviting and friendly. We had a great conversation, and I enjoyed his company. As we chatted, I noticed that Malcolm's interest in me seemed more than friendly. Time moved seamlessly from early evening to early morning, and I found myself wondering where the hours had gone. By the time I left the dinner, Richard and Malcolm had convinced me to attend a party they were throwing that evening. Knowing I had to work the next day, I struggled with my decision to attend, but I let myself be persuaded. I had one request, however: I was not driving. Richard agreed to drive me to the party and back home.

Later that day, I learned that Malcolm would be driving me instead of Richard. By this point, I had decided it didn't matter if I had to drive, so I met Malcolm at a predetermined location, decided I would drive myself, and invited Malcolm to join me for the ride. Malcolm had a lot to talk about, and he was very charming. He told me he was a police officer, and he had not only a wife but also a son. He told me about his life and the loss of his beloved mother.

He began to ask me questions about my life. He told me, among many other things, that I was sexy and he loved my voice. I'm often told this by both men and women, so his attraction did not come as a surprise, although I wondered how happy he was in his marriage to be so open with his thoughts about me. As we drove and talked, I had Alicia Keys's song "I'm Ready" on repeat. Malcolm jokingly referred to it as our song. I asked what he meant by that, but he didn't answer. The party was half an hour away, so we had lots of time to talk.

Our conversation ventured into great personal detail during the drive, and he forced me to be open to different possibilities in love and a life filled with love. Since I'd ended my last relationship after the cruise, my heart and mind had been cut off from thoughts of love. On the way to the club, we followed in my car behind Richard. Richard stopped to pick up a few people.

As we waited for them, Richard got out of the car he was driving and walked to my car. His smile was so bright, and he looked very handsome.

As he approached the car, I said, "Hey, you sexy man, you." We all had a quick chat while waiting to start our journey to the club. As we talked, the others Richard stopped to pick up got in his car.

The drive continued, and Malcolm and I returned to our conversation. As we pulled up to the club, Malcolm said, "You like Richard, and I think he likes you."

I responded, "I don't like him. I don't know him. I met him very briefly a few months ago on a cruise. Last night at dinner was the first time we had a conversation since the cruise." Malcolm found this hard to believe, but I couldn't figure out why. There was nothing between Richard and me other than the appreciation of making new friends.

The party was cool. A lot of people were there to have a good time. The night moved smoothly. Everyone was having a wonderful time, and the music was great. I did not grace the dance floor but instead talked to everyone. As the evening continued, Richard invited me to sit next to him during the female entertainment. At the time, I didn't realize this was a problem for Dana, his ex-girlfriend. She stood most of the night, but I didn't know why she was standing instead of sitting next to Richard if she wanted to do so. Apparently, it was because *I* was sitting where she desired to be. I decided to move once I realized there was friction, allowing her to sit next to Richard. I mingled with the crowd and enjoyed every second of the night. At the end of the party, I went to the back room where the entertainers were getting dressed to offer my assistance; closing the club was Richard's responsibility because he rented the club to throw the party. As I approached the back, the first person I saw was Richard. We spoke, and he hugged me, lifting me off my feet. In that moment, we shared a brief connection. The energy drew us closer in that moment, but I don't think we were aware of it then.

The drive home was filled with conversation. Malcolm rode back with me, and as we talked, the conversation became more revealing. He asked me if I found him attractive. In my mildest voice, I said, "You're easy on the eyes." This was not the response he was looking for, but it appeased him. Malcolm was a very nice-looking man with a fit body, and he had a nice smile to go along with his charm.

Richard and I had exchanged numbers, promising to keep in touch. The next morning, as I prepared to leave for a business trip, Richard called. I was surprised to hear from him so soon, but I was happy to see his name on my phone. On that call, we agreed to be friends forever and signed a verbal contract—his idea. I had never done that before and thought it was cute. We planned to hang out the following weekend when I returned from my trip.

Our first encounter as friends was certainly different because it was a last-minute decision to go to a party. I had imagined our first encounter after the party would be over lunch. Mona and I were supposed to attend a friend's party in the city, but she canceled. I didn't want to go alone, so I decided not to go at all. By now, Richard and I were communicating daily by phone, and when he asked what time I was going out, I told him I wasn't, because Mona had changed her mind. He said he would go out with me, and he offered to drive. I agreed. We had a blast! We danced a little, talked, and enjoyed the scenery at the club. Many people thought we were together, and we found ourselves saying all night that we were just friends. We found this funny, but we didn't let it stop us from having a good time and taking selfies.

After the party, we rode home full of conversation. We talked about everything; we were very open and told our stories, something neither of us would typically do. We talked until five o'clock the next morning. Time had escaped us, as we were engulfed in getting to know each other; after all, we had signed a contract to be friends for life. The conversation fed my soul and started a real friendship. This was our first time since the cruise being together without a lot of people around. Although it was five o'clock, we were still engaged in full conversation when he got a call from his ex-girlfriend Dana. I ended the evening, and we said our goodbyes.

The following week, we decided to hang out Friday night. We had spoken to each other all week on the phone and had planned to hang out at some point that weekend. I hadn't expected it to be Friday, because I had traveled all week for work and was tired; however, I was happy to see him. I suggested we chill at my place, because I didn't want to be out and about. This was different for me; I had never invited anyone to my home before, but I trusted him and felt very comfortable with him coming over. He had one request: he asked if I would read to him. This was an unusual request. No one had ever asked that of me, and it was something I had always wanted to do in my previous relationships. Needless to say, I found his request intriguing.

When he arrived, I had already selected a book of quotes that I often read. I had chilled a bottle of Moscato, as we were both light drinkers. I had also taken out my Scrabble board. This was my favorite board game, and I was hoping he would want to play. When he arrived, I was happy to see he was dressed casually, as I was. He greeted me with a big hug and a smile, as always. We talked and laughed. We played Scrabble, and as promised, I read to him. I read from my preselected book quotes by legends such as Abraham Lincoln, George Washington, and Mother Teresa. Afterward, we fell back into amazing, deep conversation, talking about life and happiness. That night, it became clear to us both that we had a powerful connection.

We saw each other every day after that, kept apart only by my business trips. For the next few weeks, we hung out and watched movies. Two movies in particular were turning points for us: *Avatar* and *The Notebook*. As we started to grow closer in our friendship, which was completely innocent and without any physical interaction, I reminded myself that he was living with his ex-girlfriend, which seemed to be a mess. It was a weeknight when we watched *Avatar*, a movie we had both seen and loved. This was the first night we balanced on the thin line between friendship and intimacy. We lay on my couch together, and he held me from behind as we watched the movie. I could feel his breath on my neck and his hands caressing my arms, waist, and stomach. While this was alarming, it also felt right and good to my soul, which had been broken, and which, without my noticing, was now experiencing a new feeling I had not felt in the past. We talked at the end of the movie but not about the closeness we had shared during it. It was an easy conversation. We were comfortable in the space we shared, and we were both unwilling to allow anything to hinder our friendship, which was becoming stronger by the day.

We watched *The Notebook*, one of my favorite movies, a few nights later. It was a cold night in January, and it was perfect for the best love story ever told. Everything was in place, and I was ready for his arrival. The only damper on the evening was that it was his ex-girlfriend's birthday. I didn't concern myself with her birthday; however, I did feel bad that she was alone. I did not ask any questions because I did not want to be nosy. Although they were no longer in a relationship, they still lived together, which meant there was more than enough baggage there for my entire neighborhood.

I watched the movie as if I had never seen it before, and he watched it as if it were the most intense love story he had ever seen. We lay on the couch together and shared a closeness that was more intimate than when we watched *Avatar*. What I have failed to mention is that Richard is a true romantic; it is a part of his being. After the movie, we talked as we normally would and shared our thoughts about different parts of the movie. It was getting late. Somehow during our conversation he was on top of me. We shared our first kiss and lovers' embrace. It was the most intimate experience I had ever shared with anyone; he touched my inner feelings, as I touched his. We kissed and caressed each other for the next hour. We allowed our bodies to connect without taking anything off. His hands explored my body as he continued to kiss me intensely. We had passed the line of friendship and connected physically. Our souls had linked without asking permission from either of us.

While we enjoyed each other, my cell phone rang several times, but that wasn't unusual, so I didn't feel the need to answer. After it started ringing continuously, I decided to see who was calling. I was becoming concerned, and I hoped nothing had happened to my parents or to anyone I loved. I did not recognize the number on my caller ID.

Richard asked me what the number was, and as I started to tell him, he finished it. Then my doorbell rang. "It's Dana," he said. We looked at each other blankly for a few seconds.

I was shocked. I had never been in a situation like this. As he began to pull himself together, I heard knocking on my front door. Although this was one of the best nights of my life, it was also one of the worst. I hadn't known what I was getting myself into, and the drama Richard had brought to my doorstep was out of character for me. Now there was an angry woman banging on my door. I said to Richard, "This is my home—my space—and this place is private. You have allowed drama to come here." It was winter, and the snow was at its peak. He asked me to allow him to go out alone while I stayed inside. "No," I said. "She's calling my name, not to mention she's at my door." He finally convinced me to let him go alone.

When he went outside, I could hear her yelling and crying. "It's my birthday," she said. "How could you be here with her on my birthday?"

Richard responded, "I told you I was going out and wouldn't be home this evening. I took you to dinner last night to celebrate your birthday."

As she yelled, my neighbors came outside, and by now, they were worried, because they had never seen this type of foolishness at my home. My neighbors thought very highly of me and were supportive. One of them called the police. I remained in my home, as Richard had asked me to do. At the time, I didn't understand why I did this, but now it's clear: I didn't want to make it worse for him. It was already the worst situation I could imagine myself in. Finally, the police arrived and asked them both to leave. The nightmare was finally over. I did not sleep well that night, as I had much on my mind. I had become intimate with someone who still lived with his ex. My home had been jeopardized, and my heart was in the middle of it all. I once again found myself moving slowly around my own broken decisions.

1

THE BEGINNING

I was born in Atlanta, Georgia, as Rachel Reynolds, daughter of Willis Miner and Anna Reynolds. I was born a bastard, as many kids from my neighborhood were. My life is what some would call a work of art or a blessing of God. At night, we were able to hide from what the world clearly saw during the day, but evil does its best work at night, targeting those no one chose to see in the daylight. My earliest memory is sitting in my grandmother's home wondering what had happened to my own home—the home my mom and I had shared and at which my father would show up a few nights a week. I was in the second grade, the age when many kids start to gain an understanding about life and their surroundings. While deep in thought about the loss of the only home I had ever known, I knew in that moment that I would be a businesswoman in corporate America with a career that would erase the fear of losing my home. I knew that I would grow up and become a provider.

I had two parents who were drug addicts, my father had lots of children by many different women, and practically my entire family participated in some type of illegal business. Things had gotten really bad in the home I once knew. Some nights, there would be different people in the kitchen with my mother getting high, and on other nights, I would hear my father beating my mother. My father was addicted to crack cocaine and had abused my mother most of my life, and my mother was always weak and allowed him to beat her. School was my home away from home, my savior. When I was in the classroom, the things that happened in my home seemed to go away temporarily. I did very well in school and did not have the worries of most kids who came from a broken home like mine when it came to performing in the classroom. I never worried about my grades, because school kept me safe.

When my mother and I arrived at my grandmother's home, six other people were living in the three-bedroom trailer already. My mother and I made eight. I immediately felt like an outsider, as I looked and spoke differently. When I spoke, I used complete sentences and correct English but my family spoke broken English. Often they would call me white girl. It was clear very early on that I was different from the others who lived in my new home. We were a dysfunctional family starting from the very top—my grandmother herself, who was money hungry. My uncle was an alcoholic who lived in my grandmother's house his entire life; my aunt was addicted to crack cocaine and would sleep with any man for a hit. My mother had been on her own since the age of seventeen and was the child with the most potential, but she was now a crackhead. My male cousin, who was only a few years younger than I, had been troubled from a very young age; his two sisters had been shown only one way of life and were already picking up habits that would lead to jail, drugs, or pregnancy; and finally, there I was, the outsider who had just moved in. I was the oldest of the children and the only person living in the home who did not have a brother or sister to call my own. Now I was another creature who had to adapt to new surroundings to survive.

I learned later that my mother had been forced to leave the apartment we lived in because her drug addiction had taken over. I had been alone many days and nights in the apartment with no food, but I had never shared a bedroom or my clothing. As I began to fit in as much as I could on the surface, I lost myself in my thoughts.

The school year had started shortly after our move, and I was in the third grade. More than anything, I was looking forward to going to school, as it was my true outlet. By this time, I rarely saw my mom because her drug habit had become worse, and I did not see my dad at all anymore. I felt as if they both had left me and never looked back, and I missed my parents' love and touch. I missed the trust I'd had that they would be there to protect me. I no longer had these things, and I learned to deal with losing so much by wrapping it in anger. My soul was broken, and I saw no way to heal it. It had been lost in the shuffle of coping.

Although I did not see my parents, I saw my grandmother daily. I remembered her being a nice lady when she would come visit me at my old home. She would spend time with me, talk to me, and buy me nice toys. But she was a totally different woman in her own house. She was mean, and she would fuss and yell frequently. My uncle was very similar to his mother. When he would become intoxicated, which was every day, he too would fuss and yell. My uncle was also abusive. He would come home drunk, hit me, and throw my things around. My aunt was in a relationship with a local drug dealer, who was abusive not only physically but also mentally. My mom and aunt had a lot in common in their personal lives, and I wondered if their mother's influence had anything to do with that. My mom and aunt were not in the house much, and there was never enough food for the kids. My things would constantly go missing. My cousins would steal my clothing, leaving me with nothing to wear of my own, and some days my grandmother would take my things from me and give them to the other kids. I did not understand, because my mother had taught me it was wrong to steal. I was trapped in a maze. I spent many days crying alone and hoping I would wake up from this bad dream. But the nightmare continued, and I lived it every day.

For some reason, my grandmother treated me differently from the other children, but she also treated my mother differently from my aunt and uncle. I would tell my mother when I saw her, but when she came in, she was always very tired and hungry. My mom did not believe me when I told her the things that were happening when she was away, as she was still trapped in denial from my grandmother mistreating her as well. On Saturdays, my grandmother washed everyone's clothes, but never mine. She would say to me, "Your mama needs to wash your clothes, not me." My grandmother made me go with her to the Laundromat every Saturday. She never gave me a choice, but she never made the other kids go. When we returned from the washer, it would already be dark, and I could not go out and play. I would wash what I could myself so I would have clean clothes to wear to school. On Sundays, my grandmother would iron my cousins' clothes, but she never ironed mine. She would tell me I was old enough to take care of my own things. I was trapped in hell. I often thought it was a lot for a third grader, but perhaps not. I never understood why she treated me so differently, but I had accepted that this was just the way it was for me. I thought I must have been a bad girl along the way, and I was getting what I deserved. After all, my mother and father *had* left me there.

Throughout my elementary years, I focused on my studies. I got involved in everything, and all my teachers loved me. They showed me daily that they cared, something that was missing from my home life. I always worried that my teachers would ask me questions about my home life, but they never did. I began to use more and more of my energy on the things I could control. Our next-door neighbor, Ms. Ann, took an interest in me during this time, and she taught me how to fish. She would also assist me with my homework when needed. She treated me like I was special, as if I were her own grandchild, and I would play with her real grandchildren. She was the only person to ask me for my report card, and no one other than Ms. Ann asked about my homework. I was an A student, and excelling in the classroom was the one thing I controlled in my young life. Ms. Ann and I would plant flowers, and sometimes I would watch her cook.

One Christmas Day, Ms. Ann's grandson got a basketball hoop and a basketball for his Christmas gifts. My mom was in jail, and my grandmother could afford only to buy the other kids gifts, so I didn't receive any gifts. I was not sad, as God was in my spirit even then. Although not purchased for me and not wrapped in pretty paper, that basketball hoop was my gift as well. I went outside and asked Tom, Ms. Ann's grandson, if I could play with him. He said yes, and in that moment, my first-class ticket out was given to me. I played daily and became very good. I played only with the boys, because there were no girls to play with. This made me stronger and quicker than most girls at the middle-school level. I was a superstar on my middle-school team, and I was looking forward to carrying my skills to the varsity level in high school.

I had made a lot of friends, and I was ready for high school. During the summer before high school, I started to see my father more. Often, my dad and I would talk about basketball and sports in general. My father was a huge sports fan, and my new love was basketball. By now, I was accustomed to the abuse in my grandmother's home and all the things that came with living there. My dad came to pick me up a few nights out of the week, which helped tremendously. In the middle of the summer, I met Mark Rents, an old family friend. Mark had grown up with my mom, and my grandmother knew his mother well. Mark's basketball knowledge was beyond anything I ever could have imagined. He had played professional basketball for the New York Knicks for one season before blowing his knee out. Mark had come back to Atlanta for work and found himself teaching me the game of basketball. That summer, Mark trained and groomed me for high school. He would pick me up at eight o'clock each morning, and we would play ball until late evening. We would go from gym to gym around the city, and he would make me play in pickup games with older players. My job every day was to use what he had taught me in the game against my opponents.

RAQUEL M. R. THOMAS

I still remember my first pickup game. It was at Lakeview Park, and there was a game already going when we arrived. But someone was hurt, and Mark convinced the young women to let me play. They didn't want to, because I was significantly younger, and they had never seen me play before. I got in the game, but before I went in, Mark said, "This is your game now."

I got the ball to bring it up the court, and my defender was playing off me. She said, "What you got, kid? What you going to do?" I looked her in the eyes, and I pulled up for the three-pointer. I knew when it left my hands that it was good. I felt its rotation when I came out of my tuck, and I looked at the ball in the air, still holding my shooting arm high in the sky. All I heard was *swoosh*!

I looked at Mark. He said, "This is your game, and no one here can check you." My confidence became fierce then; I had become a true competitor on the court. Many people knew who I was from the pickup games that summer, and I made more friends through basketball. I was officially ready to start my freshman year.

2

SOUL-SEARCHING

Entering Westside High School was great. It seemed that my home life was becoming happier and more peaceful. My grandmother and I had developed a friendship over the summer, and she would often ask me about my day and how basketball was going. She was more interested in me as her grandchild, and it felt good. She knew how excited I was to start at Westside, and she encouraged me to play ball. My mom and I had continued to grow apart during this time of my life, but my father and I were becoming even closer. I started to refer to my grandmother as Granny, as the other kids did. I had always wanted to call her that but had been afraid to. I felt less than the other children, so I didn't refer to her the same way they did. My granny became my supporter at home, and my father was my supportive parent away from home. Although things were still crazy in the house with fighting, drinking, and drugs, my granny found the time to talk to me and to listen to my basketball stories.

The first sport of the year was volleyball. A few of my friends were trying out and asked me to do the same. I was unsure, because I had never played before, and I didn't know what to do; however, I thought it would be a good idea to get in shape for basketball season, and the volleyball coach was also the basketball coach. Tryouts went well, and I caught on quickly. I was more athletic than the other underclassmen, and I did a pretty good job of keeping up with the seniors. My coach told me I was a natural. During volleyball tryouts, it became obvious that I was special. Tryouts were over at the end of the week, and I made the girls' varsity volleyball team. My partner during practice was a senior by the name of Shanae. She was tall and thin. She was one of the best players on the team, and she took pride in working with a younger player who had talent. We became best friends and had a great volleyball season. I got a lot of playing time among our senior superstars, and they all seemed to respect my athleticism, although many of them did not like that I was cutting into their playing time. We played in the championship game that year and lost. I felt horrible, as this was the last year for the seniors, and they had not come away with the championship. But my sadness soon turned to happiness, because it was time for basketball season.

During basketball tryouts, I played well and showed my stuff. I knew I would make the team, but what I did not know was that I was going to play junior varsity. I was devastated and hurt. I felt that I had failed myself; deep down, I knew I was supposed to play varsity. I felt trapped in failure and as if I had lost everything. Shanae encouraged me, and she was very positive about my situation; however, she was on varsity. I felt even more upset by this, because I was a better player than she was. Coach Gwen heard how upset I was and called me to her office. She told me she'd had to put me on junior varsity, because they would not have had any help otherwise. She said I was not only on junior varsity but also varsity. That made my heart smile, although I could not show it on the outside, as I was afraid somehow that it would all be taken away from me.

The junior-varsity season was a great success, and we won most of our games. My dad came to all my games, never once making an excuse. My mom, on the other hand, did not attend a game, as she thought basketball was for boys. My granny could never come, because she had to watch my younger cousins, but afterward, we would discuss each game. All the varsity girls came to the games, along with the coach, to support the team. This made me feel as if I had a family. My varsity game nights were even better. I played just as much as the starters, and I was playing good ball. During this time, Shanae and I became even closer in our friendship.

There was also a guy named John who played on the boys' varsity team, and he always made time to speak to me and offer me a ride home. John was a junior, and he was also a superstar on the football team. Everything was going well in school and with sports. My social life was wonderful, and I had a best friend to confide in.

At home, I had found ways to keep money in my pocket and to take care of myself financially. All my male cousins participated in some type of illegal occupation, and I happened to be their favorite little cousin. They all provided me with cash and bought me nice clothes and shoes, as did my dad, who was always around now to provide the things I needed. My mom not only used drugs but was also a drug dealer, and although I never saw her, she did a good job of providing me with the material things I needed. I was very fortunate in this way. I often gave my granny money to take care of things in the house. During the week, Coach Gwen would spend time with me, teaching me about things in life that were so different from what I saw in my home and neighborhood. Shanae and I hung out often, and we always made time for each other. John was always around to provide me with transportation and hang out with me.

The school year was a great success. My grades were good, and the basketball team was preparing for the Christmas tournament in Macon, Georgia. I was excited and ready to play the teams we had not faced during the season. On this trip, I realized not all girls were attracted to boys. This was the first time I had ever stayed away from home, and it was a learning experience. I was unaware that some of my teammates were interested in girls, but to be honest, it didn't bother me one bit. These were still my teammates, and I loved each of them the same, no matter their sexual preferences. The term used in high school for this was *dyke*, which was equal to someone calling you a bitch or ho. What confused me the most was that some of my teammates had boyfriends.

On the second night of the trip, Shanae asked me if I liked girls.

I told her no.

She said, "I think you do, but you just don't know it yet." I remember feeling uncomfortable, as I had never thought about girls or boys outside of John.

After giving it some deep thought and listening to Shanae go on and on about the team, I asked her if she liked girls.

She said, "I like *a* girl, but I don't like girls."

I told her it was OK if she liked girls; I said I would still love her—she was my best friend. The conversation ended, and we went to sleep. The tournament was a great success; we won the championship and went home with the trophy in hand. It was my best game of the season, and it set the tone for my high school career.

After basketball season, there were soccer and track and field, neither of which I had ever participated in. I decided to try out for both sports, as I wanted to stay in shape for basketball the following season. I ran track with Shanae and John, so I spent more time with both of them; however, I played soccer alone, without any of my former teammates from volleyball or basketball. I learned a great deal from both sports, and they kept me away from my home life, which was becoming more difficult.

My mom was coming in late at night more often, always drunk and high. My nights were restless, and I frequently didn't get enough sleep for the next day of school. I started to become ill and had minor problems with stress around this time. My granny took me to the hospital, and the doctor said I had ulcers. She suggested I see a therapist to help me sort out the stressful things in my life. I could tell by the look on my granny's face that she did not want me to see a therapist. There were a few reasons she did not believe in therapy, but mainly, it was her lack of education about the proper mental health care needed in situations like mine. I knew for sure that she did not want me to discuss my mother, my aunt and uncle, or drugs and alcohol. Before we left the hospital, the doctor scheduled my first appointment with the therapist.

When we got in the car, my granny said, "If this will help you, then I will make sure you get to the doctor. You are different from the other children, and you're going to make it out of here one day. Just don't forget about your old granny."

I looked at her, smiled, and said, "I would never forget you."

When we arrived home, we found that my mother was back from a six-day drug getaway. She asked how the appointment went, but I didn't respond. My granny told her I had ulcers and that they could kill me if didn't stop stressing so much. She also said the doctor made an appointment for me to see a therapist to help me sort out the stress. My mother immediately looked at me and said I'd better not tell the doctor about anything that went on in the house. I felt scared, but most of all, I didn't know how ill I was at that point or if the ulcers really could kill me. I remember the doctor saying that fifteen was young for a child to have several ulcers. I didn't respond to my mother's comment about the doctor, but it did make me very angry on the inside. I felt like she was only worried about herself and what trouble she would get into.

As promised, my granny took me to my first appointment with the therapist. My mother also decided to go with us. Before we got out of the car, my mother said to me once more, "You better not tell that doctor about nothing that goes on in the house."

I felt as if I was wasting everyone's time. As I walked into the room with the therapist, my mother tried to enter with me, but the therapist stopped her. I was very nervous and scared, because my mother's normal behavior was to fight and to use profane language. To my surprise, my mother was very nice and sat back down. I was even more confused and nervous.

I didn't say much in the session, as I did not want to get into trouble or to get anyone else into trouble at my house. When the session was over, the therapist asked if anyone had told me not to talk. I looked at her without responding. She told me she couldn't help me if I didn't talk to her.

"Ma'am, no one can help me," I said and walked back out to the waiting room. I never went back to therapy, because I was afraid and knew I couldn't say anything. My mom asked me what I'd said, and I told her I'd said nothing.

I took the medication the hospital had given me, and I got better over time. I never mentioned this to anyone, not even Shanae. I never talked about my home life, and no one had any reason to question it. There were a few kids who knew both of my parents were drug addicts, but no one ever said anything to me about it, because the kids who knew also had one or both parents on drugs. Sometimes I felt as if some of my friends' parents and my coaches felt sorry for me and wanted to help me, because they knew my parents were in the streets.

The school year was coming to an end, and we were approaching prom. John had asked me to go with him, but my mother said no, because of my age. I was cool with her decision, as I thought only about preparing for the next basketball season. One day, when Shanae was at my house, we were talking about her prom. She was so excited, even though her boyfriend was a creep who often physically and mentally abused her. I always kept her secret, because she had made me promise. But I did not like her boyfriend, and I never understood what she saw in him.

My mother happened to walk into my room, and Shanae said, "Ms. Reynolds, you should let Rachel come to prom with the girls and me." I was shocked, because we had not discussed my going to prom with her, and besides, I didn't want to go. Shanae told my mom she would buy my things, because she had been saving her money from her part-time job. My mom agreed, as long as Shanae took care of me and I was home safely by midnight. Shanae smiled at me and told my mother she had a deal.

I didn't know what to say or why Shanae wanted me to go to prom with her. I knew her boyfriend wouldn't be happy, and I didn't like the idea of having to spend time with him. When my mom left the room, I asked Shanae what she was thinking and how she was going to pull it off. She told me not to worry and said she would take care of everything.

We started shopping for prom, and as promised, she purchased my things. Her boyfriend was upset that she was bringing me along with them, and he started to dislike me as much as I disliked him. One day after prom shopping, Shanae and I were sitting on the couch at her grandmother's house. "I want to kiss you," she said.

I immediately felt uncomfortable, as I did not understand where this was coming from. She said it once more and then asked me if it was OK.

I didn't respond.

She said, "If you're not gay, then it won't matter."

Finally, I said OK, and she kissed me. Afterward, I felt confused, and I asked her to take me home. She did and said she would call me. I jumped out of the car without responding.

"Are you OK?" she asked when we talked later.

"Yes," I said, "but I'm not going to prom. I don't think it's a good idea, because of your boyfriend. Besides, I don't want to go anyway."

"OK," she said. "How do you feel about the kiss? Are you mad at me?"

"I'm not mad, just confused."

"Did you like it?" Shanae asked.

"I'm not sure," I responded.

She said, "You have to know that we're closer than just friends. Look at all the time we spend together and how often we talk on the phone when we're not with each other."

It made me think, and once again I found myself confused.

3

LOVE APPROACHES ME

John and I were growing closer and enjoying our time together. He was a great guy, and he always made time for me. We played ball and worked out together. John would take me to my part-time job at the Pizza Joint most days and pick me up. He would sometimes hang out at my job while I was working, so we could still see each other. We both loved going to the movies and out to eat, and he always tried to make things better for me. We talked about sex, but very little. We agreed to wait until we were married, and that worked for both of us.

One evening after a movie, we were sitting in the car, and he said he loved me. I didn't know what to say, as I didn't hear those words often from anyone. I looked away from him, and he said, "It's OK if you don't love me. I didn't say it for you to say it back." He smiled and kissed my lips softly. "Let's get you home before I miss your curfew. I don't want your grandmother mad at me, because I'm her favorite." My curfew was nine o'clock on the weekends, and during the week, it was whenever I was done with sports.

One day after school, Shanae and I were heading to the mall. "I love you—and not like a friend," she said.

I looked at her. "What do you mean?"

She said, "I think about you at night, and when I'm with my boyfriend, I wish it were you."

"I love you too," I said, "and I think about you often as well."

"What are we were going to do about how we feel?"

"I don't know," I said. "To complicate things, John told me he loved me."

"What did you say?" Shanae asked immediately.

"I was too scared to respond, so I didn't say anything."

"Do you love him?"

"Yes," I answered. I knew this bothered Shanae, but I didn't know how to make things better, so I didn't say anything.

Sometimes love comes in different forms, and the reach to accept it is too far. I was at war with myself, and I didn't know what to do about it. John was a junior, and Shanae was a senior. They were both very popular, and both had expressed their feelings for me. I wondered how they could really love me when, at times, it felt like no one in my home loved me. I was afraid and felt like walking away from them both. I didn't want them to hurt me or leave me, as my mom and dad had done. I didn't want to become dependent on either of them, as I had become dependent on my mother as a child. I didn't want to face a day of pain that would follow if I allowed myself to fall more deeply for either of them.

I found myself pulling away from them both, but as I pulled, they both pushed closer to me. They each made me feel safe, and neither pressured me to do anything I didn't want to do. I made out with each of them, and we shared moments of simplicity, such as watching a movie on the couch. They made me a part of everything they did, and they found themselves fighting for my time as they started to demand more of it. Each became jealous of the time I would spend with the other. There were many times when we were all together, as we all ran track, and those moments were very awkward, as everyone knew I was dating John.

I knew I had to make a decision, but the truth was, I loved both of them, and they were both very special in my life. I knew they had made me their priority, and I did not want to hurt either of them the way I had been hurt many times by my parents. I wanted to protect them both, but I didn't know how. I wanted all of us to hang out together, but I knew that would never work. I was torn between them, and I didn't know what to do. Once again, my soul was broken, because I didn't know what was next or if I would lose the two people who cared for me the most.

4

FALLING APART

Early on Mother's Day, I slept lightly on the couch as my granny cleaned, just as she did every morning at five. I could hear her footsteps and the vacuum as she went from room to room. My granny and I had grown close, and we had a complete understanding of each other.

Heavy footsteps entered through the front door, along with yelling from my drunk and high mother. She had been gone for days now, which was perfectly normal. As she entered the house, she said, "Happy Mother's Day, Ma."

Granny replied, "Thanks, Anna. You need to get your life together." I heard the voices getting closer to me. My eyes were closed, but I was awake.

My mother said, "My daughter is going to be successful and get me out of here." My granny and I were silent, as we knew this could be a bad morning or a good one; we just didn't know which yet. All of a sudden, my mother grabbed me from the couch and asked me for twenty dollars. I told her I didn't have any money, but she knew my dad had been there the previous night. Saying no was the biggest mistake I could have made that morning, because I *did* have twenty dollars. I was working, and my older cousins often gave me money too. I didn't give it to her because I knew she would buy more drugs and alcohol with it, neither of which she needed.

By now, she was scaring my granny and me. "You think you're better than me, but I will fuck you up in here, because I'm the mama."

I stayed silent, hoping her rage would pass, and she would simply go back in the street, as she did most times. I finally sat up, as I could hear my little cousins moving around in the bedroom where all three of them slept. They did not come out of the room, as they were also afraid.

When I sat up, I told my mom once again that I didn't have any money. By now, she was taking my things—the things she had bought for me—and throwing them in the hallway. She asked me for the jewelry she had bought me, which I was wearing. I gave it to her and said she could have it. She knocked it out of my hand and said, "I'll show you better than I can tell you. I'm the mama, and you're no better than me or nobody else." She went outside, but I knew it wasn't over. I lay back down on the couch, and my granny continued to clean. The kids were quiet in their room, so I assumed they had gone back to sleep.

Suddenly, the door burst open, and the footsteps were even louder this time. My mom came in with a two-by-four that had been cut by some workers who were building a toolshed behind the trailer; my granny had already added a room so there was more space for our family. My mom came directly at me on the couch and swung the board. She said, "This is my child, and I will do whatever the hell I want to do to her. Don't touch me, or I will fuck your ass up too."

The beating went on for at least ten minutes. As she hit me with the two-by-four, I could see my granny looking at us, not knowing what to do to help me. My seventy-one-year-old granny stood still as the beating continued.

My body went into shock, and I didn't feel a thing. I was conscious and could see everything that was happening, but I couldn't feel or hear anything. I could see my mother's lips moving as she hit me with the board. Everything was still and quiet. I remember seeing red everywhere. I could smell my blood, and the sight of it made me wonder if I was going to die, if my time was up. I was afraid of the outcome, but I knew it was best that it was only me and not my granny or the kids.

I saw more people enter the house. The police had arrived, and four cops approached my mother.

One grabbed her by the neck, threw her to the floor, and dragged her out of the house. My angel had arrived just in time that morning. My little cousin had jumped out of the bedroom window and run to a neighbor's house to call the police. I'm sure she saved my life that day, as my granny had made no move to, and I'd had no power to help myself.

The ambulance was there by now. I was lying on the floor, and a cop said to me, "Please don't move. We're going to get you help." The paramedics entered the house and asked if I could hear them. I didn't reply, because I couldn't speak, but I could hear the questions. My eyes were open as the cops and paramedics moved around me. They gave me a shot in my backside and put me on a stretcher. When the stretcher rolled outside, there were so many people looking at my bloody body. I was embarrassed and ashamed to be in the condition I was in. As the stretcher was pushed to the ambulance, I saw my mom in the back of the police car in handcuffs, looking out the window. She was crying, and she looked as if she had been beaten as well. I saw my granny, cousins, neighbors, cops, and all the others who had come to see the show, and I felt like a zoo animal on display.

As I was lifted into the ambulance, my granny started to climb in with me. "No," they told her. "You cannot ride with her. This little girl now belongs to the state of Georgia."

I didn't know what that meant at the time. The cop continued talking to my granny. "You can follow the ambulance to the hospital. There will be more questions there."

When I arrived at the hospital, my clothes were sticking to my wounds where my blood had dried. They gave me a few more shots and asked me many questions. I still could not respond, but I could hear each question. I heard a nurse say I was in shock but still conscious. I felt the pain from the nurse cutting my clothes off me. I must have fallen asleep, because when I awoke, I didn't have on any clothes, and I was in a different room. This time, there were cops and nurses. One of the cops had a camera. "I'll need to take pictures of your wounds," he said. I lay naked, feeling violated and embarrassed as the photos were taken.

I was responsive by then, and the questions started again. I was very sore and stiff. I asked where I was. Someone replied, "You're still in the hospital. We'll have you in clean clothes shortly." The questions were all about my mom and what had happened. I asked where my granny was. A voice said my family was outside and that I could see them soon. I was in the hospital for three days, but it felt like three weeks.

I was placed in a van; I still had not seen anyone from my family, and I didn't know where the driver was taking me. When the van finally came to a stop, we were at the Department of Social Services. We entered the building from the back, and I sat in a large room with a lot of open space. I didn't know what was happening, but eventually my granny entered the room, along with several of my family members. My granny asked when could she take me home. The social worker said, "Rachel will not be going home with you or anyone in your family."

My granny said, "Well, where is she going?"

"She is now under protective care, because she has been in danger." The social worker explained that my family would not have access to me, and the court would decide where I would live and who would be granted custody of me. I felt lost and worried that my soul was broken, as I literally didn't have anything any longer. Although I hadn't had much to start with, I now had nothing.

When I arrived at the protective-care home, there were kids everywhere, and I appeared to be the oldest of them. The ride was short, and I knew exactly where we were. The home was a huge house in the city. It was in a good neighborhood; a few kids from my high school lived there. The house had seven bedrooms, and each bedroom had two sets of bunk beds.

When the social worker left, one of the housemothers took me to my room. I was silent the entire time. She said, "You'll be fine. I can tell you're different from the other kids here." I didn't know what that meant, but I figured it wasn't important, because I knew I was just like the other kids—I was in the same home they were in. She explained the rules and showed me where everything was in the house. Still, I had not said a word. After my tour, it was time for dinner. I didn't eat then, and at that point, I had not had any food in the last twenty-four hours. After dinner, the housemother told me I would leave for school at seven fifteen and needed to be dressed and ready then. All I could do was wonder how I would go to school looking like this. I went upstairs and selected something to wear. There was a huge closet of clothes, but I could tell they were hand-me-downs. I could barely find anything similar to what I usually wore, so I chose a white T-shirt and a pair of blue shorts. I knew my friends would question what I was wearing and that some might know what had happened.

I didn't sleep at all that night. I was not looking forward to going to school, but I missed my friends and family—Shanae most of all. I knew she had to be worried about me, because we had not talked for days. She and I talked all day and night if we weren't hanging out. It was very early when the van pulled up in front of my school, and most of the school buses had not yet arrived. I knew Shanae got to school around seven forty-five, but I didn't know what to say or what she would think of me. For some reason, I wasn't concerned about seeing John, though I didn't want him to see me this way. I wasn't comfortable with myself and didn't want to be embarrassed any further. As I walked into the school, I went directly to my coach's office. To my surprise, she was already there. She looked at me and asked if I was OK.

I looked back at her. "I don't know," I said. "But I do know I didn't want to wake up this morning. Today is going to be one of the most difficult days of my life." She got a call on her office phone and told me she would be right back. She asked me to wait in her office. The first bell had rung, and class had started, so I was not worried about anyone seeing me.

Coach returned and said the call was about me; the school counselor had told her what had happened. I looked down, as I did not want to face her. When I looked up, she was crying. "I'm sorry," she said.

"I'm sorry too," I said. "I'm sorry for being this way and causing problems."

She simply looked at me. "We'll get through this."

I told her I was embarrassed and didn't want anyone to see me this way. We talked, and before I knew it, the bell had rung once more; first period was over.

I decided to go to my next class, as I knew Coach Gwen had work to do. As I walked to class, my friends and classmates greeted me. I smiled back at them all and wished them good morning. My heart was so heavy that the closer I got to my classroom, the more I felt I was going to break down. I stopped at my locker and got my books.

When I closed my locker, Shanae was there. I could tell she was upset with me and expected an explanation for my not calling or meeting her at her locker before first period. When I saw her face, I immediately looked down.

She asked in her typical loud voice, "What's wrong? What happened to you? Why haven't you called or been to school? Where have you been?"

I couldn't respond, and my eyes filled with tears. She grabbed my hand, took me to the restroom, and pulled me into a stall. She asked again what had happened.

I looked up at her. "I'm living in a protective-care home. I don't know when or if I'll ever be able to go home."

She started to cry and asked again what happened. I told her what my mother did, and we cried together. In a soft voice she said, "I wish I was there with you. I'm sorry." We heard the bell ring again, and shortly after, the restroom filled with other girls. We knew we needed to leave, so we came out of the stall together and walked to Coach Gwen's office, where we spent the rest of the day. We talked and cried, not knowing what was next for me.

By the end of the day, Coach Gwen had convinced the school officials and my social worker that she would transport me home each day and take on the responsibility of spending additional time with me. The social worker allowed her to take me home after school, to practice, and to pick me up on the weekends. Somehow, Shanae and Coach Gwen got some of my things from my granny's to take back to the home with me. I didn't see John that day, and I didn't want to. I felt he deserved better than me.

The days and nights were long; the home was starting to take a toll on me. My dad had been granted weekend visits, but we had to meet at a neutral location so he wouldn't know where the home was. My dad promised he would get me out, but I had already been in the home for more than a month at that point. I had grown even closer to Shanae, and I trusted her completely with my fears, tears, and secrets. Coach was wonderful and took care of me as best she could. I had not seen my granny or family since I had been in the home, but I was allowed to call and talk to them. When I called home, everyone seemed back to normal, and my absence was now the norm. I could tell no one was trying to get me out of the home. My hope became nonexistent.

After being in the home for forty-four days, I learned that Shanae was pregnant and going out with one of my closest friends. I felt betrayed. My heart was broken. I didn't understand the rules of friendship or love. My soul had fallen without a trace of any of the broken pieces. I was lost and without mother, father, family, or friend. I cried most of the night, and I knew I was tired—tired of being a part of a world that didn't have room for me. I thought of all the good times I'd had with basketball and how thankful I was for the opportunity to play.

I went downstairs and asked my housemother for something for a headache. By now, they trusted me completely and always went out of their way to help me. They had grown to care for me, as I was one of their children. Without thinking, my housemother told me where the painkillers were. The cabinet contained the pain medication, as well as all the other medications they had in the house. I took three bottles of different types of pills. I had decided I did not want to live any longer, so I would do what was easy and take my life. I thought that I would simply never wake up again, that life would be over for me and easier for those around me. I no longer trusted anyone, as my one friend had betrayed me. I never thought that she would be having unprotected sex and not thinking about getting pregnant or contracting an STD. It seemed irresponsible to have sex without protection. Not to mention who wanted to have a child in high school and bring them into a situation of poverty, drugs, abuse, and alcohol. Shanae's home life wasn't like mine, but she was no stranger to hard times. It was bad enough she allowed her boyfriend to beat her like a rabid dog. I took several pills from each bottle, not knowing how many I would need to end my life.

When I awoke, I was in the hospital. My dad and Coach Gwen were there. I could not lift my head, but I could see them both. My dad was praying, and Coach Gwen was crying. I knew I had been unsuccessful in taking my life, and I was sorry to have hurt them. I felt like a failure and a disappointment. When they saw my eyes were open, they asked how I felt and if I needed anything. I said no and looked away.

Coach said, "Your dad has great news, kid."

I didn't look back at her, but she told me anyway. "When you're better and released from the hospital, you'll be able to go home with your dad. He has full custody of you now." A part of me was happy to be leaving the home, but I was also scared to live with my dad.

Life with my dad was better than before. He cooked for me and took good care of me. There were nights when he didn't come home, because he was out using drugs, but I never went a full day without seeing him. My mom was still locked up, and I had not talked to her since I was placed in the home. She wrote me a few letters and called often, but I never spoke to her. My dad did the best he could, and we got a chance to learn more about each other. I loved my dad for coming to get me as he'd said he would, and I knew I was going to be OK.

My grades were still good, but all sports were over, and it was difficult seeing Shanae. She would often try to talk to me, but I felt she'd betrayed all that we were. I would have never done that to her. She was graduating, so time was running out for us. John and I had grown closer, and we were spending a lot of time together. Eventually, I became more willing to listen to Shanae and why she had done what she did. I could never forgive her, especially because something was going on with us that was outside the friendship box and being pregnant did not fit. She asked me to be her child's godmother, and I said yes. I knew I would do my best, despite how I felt about Shanae and our friendship. She had become more like a long-lost sister whom I didn't know much about.

The remainder of the school year went by quickly. John and I were in a good place and having fun, and Shanae and I were on speaking terms. My focus was on basketball and getting better for the upcoming season and summer camp. I would see Shanae from time to time, and we spoke a few times a week. Rumors were starting to spread about her, but I hoped they weren't true. However, it didn't matter as much as it once had, because she was a chapter I was ready to close.

When the new school year began, I was a godmother. John had needed only a few more classes to complete high school, and he had taken them over the summer so he could start college in the fall. He was enjoying the college experience, and Shanae was also in college. By now, I didn't speak to Shanae at all and saw her only when she was at the house when I went to see Morgan, my godchild, who was with her grandmother or other family members. Things had gotten back to normal otherwise. My grades were good, and sports were going as planned. I had made new friends, and my dad and I were still enjoying our time together. I spent most of my time outside of sports preparing for college and my future. I knew I was going to leave Georgia and never return. My mind was made up. I wanted to leave everything behind and start over. I wanted to erase my life and start anew.

5

DEFINING MEASURES

I had been accepted to a few colleges to play basketball. I chose to attend the University of Maryland, which I knew would have me near Washington, DC, and New York. Maryland was far away from my life back home, and I was able to escape, if only for a moment. My father was very happy that I was playing ball in college.

My mother was out of jail. Nothing had changed with her; she was still using drugs and drinking. I don't think she noticed that I was packing my things to go to college. My dad had agreed to sign the court documents giving full custody back to my mother shortly after she came home from jail. She promised him she had changed, but I knew better. It didn't matter much though, because she was so busy in the streets doing drugs that I didn't have to see her much. To me, she was not there, and she was too afraid to ever hit me again for fear of going back to jail. Needless to say, we didn't have a relationship, and for me that was much easier, because I no longer was being abused emotionally, mentally, or physically.

On move-in day, I got to my dorm room early, and I was the only one there. My roommate had not arrived yet, and I was thankful to be able to select my side of the room first. My roommate was from Florida and my basketball teammate. I toured the campus to become familiar with it. Maryland was a large school, and I feared getting lost, but I knew I would learn my way around soon enough. I stopped by the gym to see where we would practice and play our games. It was refreshing to be in my new home and to escape my childhood. I was looking forward to getting on the court. Moving into the dorm was different, though; I'd thought I would be excited, but I wasn't. Instead, I felt empty and alone. I was happy John was coming to visit me in a few weeks. By then, I would have met all my teammates.

Practice was going well, but it was hard work and didn't compare to high school ball. We practiced twice a day—at five in the morning and again at three. We went to class in between practices, and we studied after practice each day. My new teammates seemed really cool, and we were all excited about the upcoming season. I didn't talk much to any of my teammates other than on the court or as needed. My coach seemed cool but different from when she recruited me, which was fine with me. I just wanted to play ball and get an education. I wasn't there to make friends.

John visited, and I was very happy to see him. He was doing well in college and enjoying the experience. He had great stories, and he loved being a college student. Although I didn't feel the same joy about college, I was very happy he was having fun. We talked and laughed. I shared my experiences with him and showed him around campus. I didn't have a car, so John came to see me as much as he could, which was often enough. Given the distance between us, with him in school in Georgia and me in Maryland, we saw each other more than I had expected.

School was hard, and basketball kept us all out of class during the season. It was difficult keeping up with schoolwork while playing ball. I was falling behind in my studies and knew that at some point, it wasn't going to be good. I wasn't really enjoying basketball as much as I'd thought I would, either. My coach often gave me a hard time, telling me I needed to talk more. My teammates were cool, but everyone was in their own world. We played two to three games a week and practiced nearly every day we did not have a game. I was falling behind not only in the classroom but also financially. I didn't have spending money for food, clothes, or anything I needed outside of basketball. Coach Gwen helped me a lot, but I felt horrible calling her every time I needed something—or I should say my mother called her whenever I needed something.

My dad's drug addiction had gotten worse, and he was no longer supporting me financially.

I got a job at Foot Locker to support myself. My manager loved basketball and had played in college too, so he worked around my basketball and class schedules. I worked twenty to thirty hours a week, and I was burned out. I was tired from class, studying, basketball, and working. My coach was still giving me a hard time, and my grades were horrible. I was near academic suspension. My body and mind were tired. I wasn't eating properly. I didn't have the energy or time to study. I barely had time to talk to or see John. I had no time for myself, let alone a relationship.

John was very understanding of my schedule, as he always had been. He gave me money when he could to help with the things I needed. My dad somehow was able to get me a car, which helped greatly in getting back and forth to work. Catching the bus or bumming a ride was hard some days. But with the car came insurance, which was very expensive and took most of my paycheck. As always, John found a solution to help me. He told his father my situation, and his dad offered to pay my car insurance each month to help me. I was grateful and accepted his offer. I was beginning to feel broken and as if there was no hope. Things seemed to get more difficult, despite how hard I worked.

We were midway through the season and winning games. One Sunday, I was tired before we even started practice. We were doing a two-on-three-person drill when it happened: while running the play, I felt my leg give out. For a few weeks before that practice, I had felt a sharp pain in my right leg, but I figured it was fine. When my leg gave out, it was because I had fractured the entire front of my right leg. After the team trainer evaluated me, he sent me to the local hospital. There I learned that I was out for the remainder of the season. My eyes immediately filled with tears. While my coach was hard on me, and I was tired, I could not imagine my life without playing ball. A piece of my soul had been taken from me.

Monday morning, as I hobbled to class on crutches, I felt lost. I didn't feel like going to class, but there was no way I could miss it with my grades falling. As I waited for class to start, my professor told me I needed to go see my adviser, and I thanked him for relaying the message. He began to walk away, but when he saw I was still sitting, he said, "I'm sorry, but you need to go now."

My stomach was in knots as I walked to my adviser's office because I was already on academic probation; I knew my grades were suffering as the semester was coming to an end. When I arrived, she had a few students in front of me, so I had to wait. When it was my turn, she took my student ID and pulled up my account. She said, "Due to your grades, you will be going home on academic suspension for a semester if you don't finish with a 2.0 GPA. You can return after sitting out a full semester."

I was at a loss for words and didn't know what to do. I sat for a moment to gather myself before I left her office. It was a long walk to my dorm. I thought about going home. I knew I wasn't going to finish the semester with a 2.0 because I had already gone to all of my professors to find out how to pull my grades up. I was going to finish the semester with a 1.9 GPA. I had failed, and college was not an option—at least for a few months. I called my coach and told her what had happened. To my surprise, she already knew. I couldn't figure out why she hadn't told me herself. This meant my scholarship to play ball was gone too. I had left high school with a 3.9 GPA, and I had a 1.9 GPA in college.

I returned to my dorm and began packing. I wanted to leave before my roommate came back and asked where I was going. I was ashamed and disappointed in my failure as a student. God seemed to have forgotten about me. I was broken and lost. I didn't know what I would do next. I had no idea how to tell anyone from home that I was on academic suspension *and* couldn't play ball for the remainder of the season due to an injury. I struggled but managed to get all my things to my car, my leg killing me in the process. I called my manager to tell him I had to return home and thanked him for hiring me. I knew I was never going back to the store or to the University of Maryland.

It was a long drive home, but I finally made it early Tuesday morning. It was a warm day, and the birds were singing. I hadn't told my grandmother I was coming home, so when she saw me, she was happy and surprised. We sat down on the porch and talked. Finally, she asked simply, "Are you going to be home awhile?"

I looked at her as my eyes filled with tears. "Yes, Granny. I'll be home awhile." She never asked why, and I never told her. I stayed in the house day and night, trying to figure out how I was going to tell my dad or face anyone with this disappointment. I pondered staying in the house and never coming out, but I knew I had to get a job and figure out my next move.

I woke up the next morning and went directly to the mall. My old manager had called in a favor for me, and I was hired at a Foot Locker in town. I was thankful to have one obstacle tackled. Now it was time to call my dad. Although I didn't want to do it, I knew I had to. I had no idea what I would say or how. I was disappointed in myself and my failure to maintain the grades needed to remain in school. I also had to break the news to him about my injury.

As I drove to my granny's house, I called my dad. When he picked up, I could hear the smile in his voice, because he knew it was me calling. "Hey, baby girl. How are you? Daddy misses you."

"Hey, Dad. I miss you too. Where are you? I'm coming to see you." My dad told me his location without asking any questions. When I arrived, he was working hard as always on his job. My dad worked for himself as a landscaper. We embraced, and the look on his face made me even sadder. He was so happy to see me, and I didn't want to ruin that, but I knew I needed to tell him I was home from school and wasn't sure if I was going to return.

We sat and chatted awhile about everyday matters until he finally asked, "Why are you home? Did something happen?" I said yes and looked away. I felt the tears coming, and I didn't want to cry. I was tired of crying. I explained the sequence of events to my father and told him my GPA was a hundredth of a point away from where it needed to be. I told him I had never missed class and did all my assignments, but it was hard to study, play ball, and work.

He looked at me and said, "That's OK. We all fall short sometimes, and you work hard. I should have been there so you didn't have to work, go to school, and play ball."

I told him it was my responsibility. I was nineteen years old and needed to be able to take care of myself; it wasn't his fault. I was still turned away, because I knew if I looked at him, I would cry. As we sat in silence, I glanced at my dad and saw he was crying. I asked him what was wrong as I started to cry myself.

He said, "You're a great kid, and I see so much of myself in you. You never give up. I should have been there for you. You were going through a lot by yourself. Your mom and I are lucky to have you, and you shouldn't have to work and go to school full-time while playing a sport full-time. Basketball and school are your jobs. I've failed you by not providing for you."

We sat in silence awhile. Finally, my dad asked where I was staying and invited me to live with him. He also asked about my future plans. I told him I had already gotten a job, but I wasn't sure what was next.

He smiled. "You'll figure it out. I'm sure of that."

I had been home for months, and still no one really knew I was there. I worked ten-hour days most of the week. I picked up as many hours as I could, and I worked for everyone who called out. I spent 90 percent of my time working. I had cut all communication with John, because I didn't want to face him. This did feel odd because John's father was still paying my car insurance. One day, an old friend came to the store and was surprised to see me. She asked if I was still playing ball and if I wanted to play pickup games two nights a week. By now, I had not played in a few months, and my leg was feeling better. I took the information she had given me and decided that maybe I would go play if I wasn't working.

The following Tuesday, I was off work. I had worked twenty-one consecutive days, and it was good to have a day off. My granny was at church, and I was home alone. I had run all the errands I needed to, and I was bored out of my mind. I saved most of my money, because I knew I was going to move soon. I also wanted to be in a better position financially when summer was over. There was no one living with my granny other than my uncle, and he was never home. Things certainly had changed; when I was growing up, there had always been at least six people living in my granny's house at any given time. My cousins were all grown up or living with my aunt, who had given up drugs a few years ago. That left my uncle and my granny in the house. It was great not having to share my space or worry about not having any hot water left because so many people had to shower. The thought of that made my skin crawl. I needed to get out of the house, so I dressed and found the information about playing pickup ball at the gym. The pickup games were on Tuesday and Thursday evenings, so I decided to go.

I arrived at the gym, and to my surprise, it was jam-packed with players and observers. I felt a sense of relief, like I was home. As soon as I walked into the gym, I heard a few people say my name. A few others called, "Rachel, you want to jump on my team next?" I smiled, ran over to the bench, and got ready to play. I had a blast, but I was so out of shape. I played four games before we were off the court. I saw a lot of people I hadn't seen in a very long time. For the first time, it felt great to be home. I started requesting Tuesday and Thursday evenings off so I could play ball. I enjoyed being back on the court and interacting with people again. I hung out with some of the players on the weekends at a local club. I had not been out in a long time, and it didn't hit me that it was a gay club until months later. It didn't matter to me at all; I just hadn't realized it. It was a good time, and I was able to laugh again with people I had something in common with.

One night, I was leaving the club when I saw a girl who looked familiar, but at a distance, I couldn't determine where I knew her from. Someone stopped me to talk, and I watched as the girl drew closer, finally realizing who she was. She had been the best player at my rival high school. I remembered she was difficult to defend. Her name was Addison. She and her friends were laughing and talking. I couldn't help but notice her looking in my direction the entire time I was talking. I didn't think much of it, and when I wrapped up my conversation, I headed for the door. There were a few people in front of me to get out. When I finally exited, I glanced behind me, and Addison was standing there. She smiled, and I said hi. She said, "You're the girl everyone keeps talking about."

"What does that mean? Is it good or bad?"

"Not good," she said, and we both laughed and walked out together.

We talked for hours, and she told me all the girls wanted to go out with me. Everyone had assumed I was gay in high school, because of my friendship with Shanae. Little had I known that everyone wanted to date me. I hadn't dated anyone in a long time and barely thought about it. As we continued to talk, I realized the sun was coming up, and we were still in the parking lot. I had to get ready for work, so I asked for her number and told her I would call her after work if that was cool.

She smiled. "Yes, silly! We just talked for hours, and you ask if you can call me."

I laughed too, and we exchanged numbers.

When I got to work, I was tired but in a good mood despite the lack of sleep. I thought about Addison all day, and I was thrilled to have made a friend. It seemed like forever since I'd had someone I could talk to. We had a lot in common. She was also home from college on academic suspension and was planning to transfer to another school closer to home. When I got off work, I called her. As I walked to my car, I saw someone sitting on the hood. It was Addison, and she was smiling. I was very surprised to see her. She asked if I wanted to grab some food, and I said sure. We drove in separate cars to a hot-dog joint nearby. We ate and talked. We laughed and shared more about who we were outside of basketball. She looked at me and said, "My friend told me not to go out with you, because she didn't want me to get hurt."

"How would I hurt you?"

"It doesn't matter. The more she told me about you, the more I wanted to know you." She then revealed that her friend had dated Shanae, and Shanae had shared a lot of information about me. It became apparent that Addison knew much more about me than I knew about her. Addison asked if I was seeing anyone, and if I was, if that someone was a girl.

"No," I said. "I'm not dating anyone, and I haven't made out with a girl in a very long time."

She laughed. "Should I ask if you're dating a guy?"

"I'm not dating a guy either. I was in a relationship, but it didn't work out."

Addison and I grew closer and spent nearly every day together after I got off work. We played pickup games every Tuesday and Thursday. We enjoyed each other, and I could tell we were feeling something more than friendship. I was scared, and I honestly didn't want to find out what that something was.

One evening, Addison picked me up from my granny's house. We had decided to ride to the gym together because we were hanging out after the game. When we got to the gym, it was jammed as always, but we knew we were up to play first. As I was getting my sneakers on, I heard a familiar voice. I looked up and saw Shanae. I didn't speak but instead looked back down and tied my shoelaces.

I went to the floor and stood next to Addison. I could tell she was bothered, so I asked her what was wrong.

She said, "Did you know your girl was coming out here?"

I said no and explained that I had not spoken to Shanae in more than a year. I saw my godchild weekly, but Shanae was never there. I was just as surprised as Addison. I said, "Let's play ball and have fun. Forget she's here." We looked at each other, laughed, and went on to play.

After the game, we were putting on our dry clothes when Shanae walked up to me and said, "You're not going to speak to me?" It frustrated me, but I said hi and kept walking. Addison had gone to the restroom, and she walked out as Shanae and I left the locker room. I called Addison's name, because I didn't want her to feel out of place or to walk away.

Shanae asked in a loud smart tone, "Is that your new girlfriend?" I didn't reply. I looked at her, told her to have a good night, and moved toward Addison. We got in the car and left.

Before Addison could speak, I said, "I didn't know she was coming, and I didn't want to know. Let's go eat." She smiled, and for the first time, she reached over and held my hand.

By the end of the summer, Addison and I had become very close and intimate. We shared not only a friendship but also a love for each other. We decided we would see only each other. Although I enjoyed spending time with Addison, I knew I had to do something different. I had spoken to Lena, an old friend from high school, and she was moving to Washington, DC. She asked if I was still in Maryland, and I told her I was back home in Georgia. She said I should move to DC, because she was there and didn't know anyone. I was honest with her and told her I knew it was time for me to move, but I had no idea where. When I thought more about the move, I realized it was a good idea. I knew the DC area, and it was time to get myself back together. When I saw Addison that night, I told her I was moving to DC to start over. I explained that I needed more than Georgia and that it was time for me to get back into school. She agreed, and we knew that with her going back to Kansas at the end of her academic suspension, we wouldn't be able to see each other like we wanted to. Addison thought she would transfer closer to home, but Kansas wanted her to come back on a full scholarship. We promised to remain friends and to be there as best we could for each other, but we also agreed not to wait on each other. That night Addison and I hung out with her younger brother, who had many friends over, playing cards and video games. His doorbell rang, and to my surprise, it was John.

It was like seeing a ghost. John and I made eye contact as soon as the door opened. We had not spoken in months, though he had called me a hundred times. He was also home for the summer but would soon be leaving for school, like Addison. He came directly to me and asked if we could talk. I said yes and told Addison I needed to step away for a moment. I could see the concern and confusion on her face. John and I went outside to be alone. We sat on the hood of his car awhile before he spoke. "How long have you been home? Why haven't you returned my phone calls? Where are you staying? Why did you just disappear?"

I took a moment to gather my thoughts. In a small voice, I said, "I was put out of school due to my grades. I'm on academic suspension for a semester. I also had an injury and had to sit out the remainder of the season. I was ashamed and embarrassed. I couldn't face you or anyone else. I've been home all summer working and trying to determine what's next in my life. I felt like I didn't deserve you or your family. You deserve better, and I'm barely holding it together."

He turned to me. "I would have helped you. I would have come to you." We continued to catch up on what had changed over the past few months. I told him I had decided to move to DC and start over. He was very supportive and encouraging. His only request was for me not to shut him out or give up on our relationship. I agreed but didn't know what relationship we had at that point. Addison came out and asked if I was OK and ready to go. I said yes. I told John I would call him tomorrow, and Addison and I got into the car. I knew she had a million questions for me, and I wasn't very eager to answer them. I knew she would be upset with me, because I had never mentioned John to her.

"Who was he, and what did you two have to talk about for an hour?" she asked.

I told her about John, and as I suspected, she was upset with me and felt like I had lied to her. I tried to explain as best I could, but it made things worse. I told

Addison I had not seen or spoken to John in months. Our night did not end well. She dropped me off at home and barely said goodbye before she pulled away. I felt horrible, and I was afraid of losing her now that she felt I had lied to her. Addison was the only person I talked to, and I had shared so much with her about my past and who I was.

When I went inside, my granny said John had called, and she made sure to mention what a nice boy he was. My granny had always had a soft spot for John. She thought he was the perfect guy for me. I didn't call John back, because I had a lot of thinking to do. I needed to determine when I was leaving for DC and where I was going to live. Addison was on my mind, and I knew John would want us to be close, like we had been before I'd shut him out.

I called Addison the next morning, but there was no answer. I asked her to call me when she was available. I went to my computer to look for apartments in DC and a U-Haul to move all my things. I found an apartment within a few hours and locked in the U-Haul. I still hadn't heard from Addison and was starting to worry. I decided to check my e-mail while I was on my computer and saw that I had an e-mail from Addison:

> *By the time you read this, I will be heading to the airport to go back to Kansas. I think it's best that we don't remain friends. I feel that*

you've lied to me all summer. John has been there all this time, and you never mentioned him. I love you, and I don't want to get hurt. I know we agreed to be friends and to support each other, but that isn't something I can do right now. I need space, and if you care about me, then please do not call or respond to this e-mail. I enjoyed our summer together and your company, and I see why Shanae and John are both stuck on you. Take care of yourself. I know you'll do well in whatever you decide. You're the strongest person I know, and what you have overcome in your short life is more than most overcome in a lifetime. Thank you for a great summer.

I respected her wishes and didn't call or respond to her e-mail, but I felt an ache in my chest that I had not felt before. I was hurt and sad. I was disappointed in myself for being a fool. I should have told her about John. The truth was that I had forgotten about him. She had become my only focus, and I'd thought she and I would somehow make things work between us.

When moving day finally arrived, I was ready. My granny was up bright and early with me, and my dad came over to see me off. I had not seen or spoken with my mother much all summer. She was around but mostly out in the street. As I was getting in the U-Haul to head to DC, my mom showed up. We were all surprised and had no idea where she had come from. She looked at me and said, "Travel safe. I love you."

I looked back at her in complete silence. I couldn't find anything to say to her. She looked like a perfect stranger, yet she also looked like my mother. I said my last goodbyes to my granny and dad, and I took off for my long road trip to DC. I was at ease with myself and felt like I was going to be OK. I was going back to school. I had transferred my job to another store in DC, paid my rent for an entire year, and purchased furniture. I was ready to move to my new place and start over. John was also very supportive, and he and I were back to talking daily.

6

BACK TO COLLEGE

I was in DC and settled. Work was going well, and I had enrolled in a junior college to take classes toward my major. I had the money to pay for three courses at the local community college, which helped greatly with getting back on track for school. I was working fifty to sixty hours a week and taking three classes. I had decided basketball was a part of my past. I needed to work full time to support myself. John and I were back on great terms, and we had picked up where we left off. He visited once a month and stayed for a few days each time. I was focused again on what was important: my education and working toward my career.

I enrolled at Howard University the following semester. I planned to finish my degree in business. I now needed more money to put myself through college, as Howard was much more expensive than the local community college. I'd had a scholarship at the University of Maryland and didn't have to worry about tuition. I had to make some decisions and knew I'd need to pick up another job to complete my degree. I got a second job working at night for FedEx, but this time, I made school my priority. The money was decent, and my night job came with health benefits, which I needed, because I didn't have insurance. While I attended Maryland, the school had provided insurance, but that had stopped when I left the university. Tuition for one semester at Howard was just under $10,000, and I was still going to be short. This meant I needed $20,000 a year to attend school, and I had two years to go to complete my degree. That led me back to the drawing board.

As I sat in my apartment with a pen and pad, trying to map out how I was going to make ends meet, my granny called. I was surprised, because she never called me; I normally called her. I could hear in her voice that she was upset about something, so I asked her what was wrong. She told me President Bush had cut her food stamps and her social security check, and she was now unable to purchase her diabetes and blood-pressure medications. This made me very angry. The government seemed to help those who were young, able, and rich but left our elderly struggling and without. I told my granny not to worry—I would send her the money she needed monthly. I could hear the smile on her face, and that made me smile. I was trying to figure out how to pay my college tuition, and now I had another responsibility. My granny had five children, but none helped her financially. They all wanted something from her, or they did not exist in her life. I felt the stress in my chest, and the worry started to sink in. How was I going to pay my tuition, take care of myself, and help my granny?

After I hung up with my granny, my phone rang again. This time I was slightly afraid to answer it, because I couldn't deal with another financial surprise. It was John. I had nearly forgotten he was coming to see me for a few days. When I heard his voice, I was excited and looking forward to seeing him. We talked every day on the phone and e-mailed each other throughout the day while at work. I could use some downtime, as well as some time away from my life.

That night, we planned to go to dinner and to a nightclub I had been frequenting. I wanted to dance and have a good time. Over the years, I had always danced, even as a small child; I danced in competitions with my cousin Keisha. I went out a few times a month to dance to let off steam. John had just finished pledging Omega Psi Phi the spring before, so he was dancing all the time. We were excited about being together and having a good time. The distance made every moment between us special.

The music was on point, and the club was packed with people dancing and having a good time. "Sexy Lady" by the go-go legend Chuck Brown was playing, and the people were going crazy! This was one of our favorite songs to dance to. After the song was over, we needed a drink. Neither John nor I drank alcohol, and it seemed we were the only people in the club who didn't. It was hot, and everyone was sweating from dancing. DC was known for go-go music since the sixties, so if you wanted to dance, DC was the place to be. We finally took a break, and John went to the bar for water. While I was waiting, a tall, handsome man approached me. In a deep voice, he said, "My wife would love to meet you. We've seen you a few times at this club." I was confused as to why this woman would send her husband to drag me over to meet her. I told him I was with my boyfriend, and I would come over when he returned. He nodded and pointed to where she was so I would know where to go once John came back.

When John returned, I told him what had happened. "Go meet her!" he said. I headed in her direction.

To my surprise, she was sitting in the VIP section, and there were a lot of people surrounding her. I started to turn around, because I didn't want to wait, but as I did so, her husband took my arm. With a smile, he said, "Where are you going?"

I followed him and sat down. She was very inviting. "My name is Tina, and this is KD. I've been watching you dance for the last few weeks, and I wanted to meet you." I asked her why, confused.

She asked, "Can I take you to lunch or dinner? I'd like to sit down and talk to you outside the club." When I didn't immediately respond, she said, "I promise I'm not a crazy person trying to kidnap you. I'll come alone and meet you wherever you'd like."

She smiled, because I was staring at her, still silent and confused. She gave me her number. "I think we can make a lot of money together. Call me, and we'll discuss all the details, but I'd prefer to talk about this face-to-face."

I took her number and said OK. As I walked away, she said, "Call me. Don't throw my number away."

I smiled and said I would call; however, I planned to throw the number away as soon as I got away from her. Eventually, I decided to hold on to it, but I was still unsure if I was going to call. She'd said we could make a lot of money together, and I hoped she didn't think I was a prostitute. I didn't see John, so I went toward the restroom, where I saw him standing in line. I waited with him until it was his turn. When he came out, he asked if I was ready to leave, and I said yes. It had been a long day but a good night.

We crashed as soon as we got in. We were both tired, and John had driven for hours to come see me. When I awoke, I cooked breakfast, and then I was back to my pen and pad to try to figure things out. When John awoke, the food was cold, but I warmed everything so we could eat. When he got to the table, he kissed me. "Good afternoon. I haven't slept this late in a very long time."

I smiled. "I'm glad you were able to rest." As we ate, I kept brainstorming.

"What are you working on?" he asked.

"I need to figure out how I'm going to pay for school and give my granny money, because she needs things back home."

His face got heavy, but I reassured him I was going to take care of it. "You're already working two jobs and going to school," he said. "How will you do more? There are only twenty-four hours in a day."

I looked at him. "I don't know, but I'll figure it all out." Then I changed the subject and put my pad away. I didn't want to waste another moment on my financial issues. Besides, John was leaving the next day, so he could prepare for college himself.

John and I decided to order in and watch movies for his last night in town. We wanted to spend as much time together as possible before he had to leave. It would be a few months before we saw each other again. We finished our movie and prepared for bed. We talked for hours and shared warm kisses and body heat. I had never had sex with a guy, and John had been with only one girl. I could tell our kisses were going to lead to something else. We were both very comfortable with each other, and we communicated well. We continued to kiss and touch. We were naked before I knew it, and I could feel his hardness against my leg. I asked him if he had a condom, and he did. He asked if I was sure I was ready, assuring me that he would wait until we were married. But I was ready, and he was my perfect guy. I told him so. We shared a night of intimacy, and although we were both inexperienced, the love we shared for each other made up for it.

Morning came fast. When I awoke, John was watching me. He looked into my eyes and said, "I love you. One day, I want you to be my wife."

I looked at him in silence. When words finally found me, I said, "You better get showered. It's almost time for you to get on the road." He smiled and said OK. When he got up, I packed his things and put some travel clothes on the bed. It was a long drive, so he needed to get an early start. We said our goodbyes, and when he started his car, I walked back into my apartment.

I was fully back to reality. I had a lot on my mind as I got ready for work. I had been accepted to Howard, and my tuition was due in two weeks. I had not heard back on my school loan request, which meant I had to come up with the money another way. After paying my bills and sending money home to my Granny, I didn't have much left for anything else. My store was slow that day, so I had time to make a few phone calls. As I did, I remembered the woman from the club. With my tuition payment looming, I decided to call and see what she had in mind to make money.

I was hoping for her voice mail, but she picked up. "This is Tina."

"Hi. This is Rachel. We met at the club a few nights ago."

"Hello. I didn't think you would call."

"Me either, but you piqued my interest." She asked if I could meet for dinner, and I said yes. "I get off work at five and can meet you at seven at the Ole Hooper." She agreed, and we hung up.

I was getting dressed and talking to John on the phone when I realized he'd never asked why the woman had wanted to meet me that night at the club. John didn't ask many questions, so I wasn't surprised. I told him I was going to dinner with a friend, and he told me to have fun and be safe. When I arrived at the restaurant, I saw Tina walking in. I was a little nervous but ready to hear what she had to say. I met her at the table, and again, she was warm and inviting. "You never told me your name at the club."

I laughed. "I'm sure you already knew my name."

She laughed too. "Yes, you're right. I did already know your name."

"What else do you know about me?"

"Not much other than your name and that you don't drink."

"How do you know that?"

"I have been watching you for weeks at the club, and you never get a drink, only water. So, I assumed you didn't drink."

"Great assumption. No, I don't drink." We ate and made small talk until I finally asked, "How can we make money together?"

"I'm a club promoter and owner. I own a gentlemen's club, and the men would love you. There's a lot of money to be made. I was hoping you would come check the club out one night and possibly consider dancing for me."

I laughed out loud. "I'm not a dancer. I've never danced in a club for money. The only dancing I've ever done was for fun."

"That's even better," Tina said. "You're a new face, and you have an amazing body to match."

"I'm sorry, but I'm in school and working two jobs. I'm not a dancer. I'm just trying to take care of myself and finish school. Thank you for considering me, but no thank you."

She said OK and then asked if we could be friends.

I smiled and said yes. "How long have you been married?"

"We're not married, he says that to be funny and territorial. KD is my dude, and we have one child together. He's an exotic dancer, and he spotted you in the club. Once I saw you myself, I had to talk to you."

Tina was a smart woman and very attached to the streets—growing up with a mother and a father on drugs, I knew the streets when I saw them. She seemed to have done well for herself as a club owner and promoter. I didn't have many friends, and I thought it would be nice to count Tina as one.

After dinner, I thanked Tina and gave her my number.

"What are you doing tomorrow?" she asked.

"I have some calls to make in the morning, but I'm off from work tomorrow."

"Cool. Do you want to hang out? I have some errands to run on this side of town tomorrow."

I said I would be free after one o'clock, and then we went our separate ways.

The next afternoon, Tina said she would pick me up, explaining it would be easier if we were in one car. I gave her my address, and she pulled up fifteen minutes later.

I had been stressing once more about my finances, and Tina could tell something was on my mind. "What are you thinking about? Do you always look so serious?"

"Yes, I think so. People tell me that a lot." I told her school was starting in a few weeks, and I had tuition to pay, but I didn't know how I was going to do it.

"Do you need more work?" she asked. "I'm sure I can find you a job."

"I already have two jobs. I don't think I have time for a third job." We both laughed. She told me to let her know if she could help, and I thanked her.

We made a few stops, and I stayed in the car for most of them. The last stop was her club. We went in, and everyone greeted her as we walked through. She had me sit at the bar and told the bartender to give me whatever I wanted. I asked for a bottle of water, and the guy smiled. "Is that it?" I smiled back and said yes.

After about twenty minutes, Tina came out to the bar. "I'm all done. Let's go. I need to get dressed for tonight. Do you want to come back out to the club with me tonight?"

"I'm not dancing."

"OK," she said, "but we can chill while I work."

She dropped me off at home so I could change. I called John to fill him in on Tina as I got dressed. He was neutral as always, and his only concern was my safety. At ten o'clock, I heard Tina's horn. I had no idea how late I would be out, so I had prepared my things for work just in case.

The club was packed by midnight. All I could see was money being thrown everywhere. Tina introduced me to all the dancers and workers. She told them I was her new best friend and not to mess with me; I was a good girl. "She doesn't drink, smoke, or use drugs, so keep all that away from her."

That made me smile, because I knew she had my best interests at heart. I could see that most of the girls and more than half the staff were on drugs.

At the end of the night, Tina said, "Now we eat."

I laughed. "It's two o'clock in the morning!"

"I know," she said, "but we still have to eat."

As we left the club, I heard Tina tell a few people to meet us at the pizza joint down the street. When we arrived, there were at least twenty people waiting. Most of them were from the club.

I saw KD, and he smiled at me.

"What are you smiling at?" I asked.

"You!" he said. "I'm happy to see you, but I'll be happier to see you dance. Tina told me you said no but that you were cool people."

I smiled. "I'm not a dancer."

In a low voice, KD replied, "But you could be."

We sat down and ordered. Everyone was talking about the night and how much money they'd made. Tina was quiet as everyone else talked. They all had a lot of questions for me. Unlike Tina, I talked a great deal, answering all the questions that were coming from the table. We finished eating, and Tina asked me if I wanted to leave. I had to work in five hours, so I was ready to go. As we walked out, everyone was smiling, almost as if they had a running joke. I said goodbye to everyone, and one girl said, "Oh, we'll see you again. You're Tina's new sidepiece."

"What does that mean?" I asked.

She said, "You'll find out soon enough."

I saw KD laugh, but Tina had no facial expression at all.

She looked at me and asked, "You ready?"

We pulled up at my apartment. "Thank you for allowing me to hang out," I said. "I had a good time with your people."

She smiled but looked very tired. As I was getting out of the car, she pulled my arm and said, "I almost forgot. Here you go."

I turned back and saw a stack of money in her hand. "What's that for?"

"It's your pay for tonight."

I was confused. "Pay? I didn't work."

"If you hang with me, then you're working. Now, take the money."

It felt wrong accepting money from anyone, let alone someone I had just met. I got back in the car. "This doesn't feel right. I didn't earn this money, and you don't have to pay me to hang out with you."

She laughed and dropped the money in my lap.

"What did that girl mean when she said I'm your new sidepiece?"

"Well," Tina said, "when I bring someone new around, I'm typically seeing them or sleeping with them."

"Does KD have an issue with that?" I asked.

Tina laughed. "Girl, no. He joins me when it's women."

"When it's women…so you have male sidepieces as well."

"Yes," she replied.

"I'm not your sidepiece, Tina, nor do I want to be."

"I know, and that makes me want you even more, but I'm cool with being friends. I like you a lot, and you're a good kid. You work hard, you're in school, and you want something beyond the streets and clubs—to me, that's cool. I want more people like you around me."

I smiled. "Well, you have me. Thank you for the money." I got out of the car and went into my apartment.

My alarm went off at seven. The morning had come quickly, and I was tired. I had stayed out too late. I got up, showered, and called John as I dressed. I told him I was OK and heading to work. I didn't want him to worry about me, because we hadn't talked since I'd left to go out the night before. It was a quick conversation. I grabbed my keys and saw the money Tina had given me on my counter. It was $500. I couldn't believe she had given me that much money. I got to my store and settled in. I took out my pen and pad and started figuring out how I was going to pay for school. I had not come up with anything different other than I now had $500 toward my tuition payment.

I was working hard and still hanging with Tina. Night in and night out, I saw a lot money being filtered through the club. Every night that I spent with Tina, she gave me a few hundred dollars. This helped me greatly, as school had started, and I was able to make my monthly tuition payments solely because of the money she gave me. I was sending $500 a month home to my granny. I used the remainder of my money to pay my bills.

One day, I was closing my store when I saw Tina waiting in the hallway. I smiled. "What's up?"

WHAT BECOMES OF A BROKEN SOUL

"Let's go eat," she said.

"Are you OK?"

She smiled and said, "I will be."

As we ate, she told me she and KD had decided to call it quits. She'd learned that he was having a baby with someone else. He had nine kids already.

I asked, "What does KD stand for?"

"King Dick!" We both laughed, and I thought this was a fitting name, given all the kids he had.

We continued to talk and learn more about each other. I asked her if she had any other businesses and said I wanted to own my own business one day. "I do have another business," she said, "and you will be a great business owner one day. I can tell. When you're with me, you take everything in, and I never have to show you anything twice."

"Thank you," I said, "but I still have a long way to go before I'm as successful as you. What other business do you have?"

Tina was silent a moment before she replied. "There was a time when I danced, and then I decided I wanted more and more. I built a good customer base while I was dancing, and eventually, I did only private parties or guest features at clubs. During the private parties, I was offered money to have sex. I turned it down for a long time until I found out how much I could make. I went from dancing in the club to doing private parties to escorting. I only take customers who can afford one thousand dollars a night with me. I dance and put on a show, and then I fuck them to sleep. So, kid, that's one of my other jobs."

I stared at her, not knowing what to say. I knew I could never sleep with men or women for money.

"Any more questions?"

"What are the other jobs?"

"Are you sure you want to know?"

"Yes," I said. "After telling me you run an escort business, I'm not sure what else you can say to shock me!"

She laughed. "Sure I can. I also sell E pills, coke, and weed."

I was surprised. I had lived around drugs all my life, and I never suspected this from Tina. I realized this was how she was able to give me hundreds of dollars a week to hang out with her. She finished her confession by also admitting that she had girls who worked as escorts for her business. That was the biggest surprise of all. "What do you mean?" I asked.

"Well," she said, "maybe the word 'pimp' would help, but I don't like that term."

"Wow. When you saw me dancing, did you think I could be pimped?"

"I didn't know, but I knew I had to find out. Now that I know you, I would never pimp you or give you drugs, but I would let you dance for me."

I laughed. "We're back to dancing again?"

A few weeks passed. School was going well, and Tina and I were getting closer. Things with John were good too. I was covering my tuition, helping my granny, and paying my bills. John was coming to visit, and I wanted him to meet Tina. Work had gotten busier, so my days and nights were long. Between school, studying, hanging out, talking to John on the phone, and work, I didn't sleep much. My grades were pretty good—I made mostly As—and things seemed to be going well.

John and Tina hit it off; they liked each other. It was funny seeing John in a gentlemen's club. I could tell it really wasn't his thing, but he was never judgmental. He was always down for anything with me. John stayed for a few days, as always, and then he had to go back to school. John and I were getting busier with our lives in different states; college, work, and the distance were difficult. As he gathered his things to leave, I said, "The distance is putting a lot on us both. We miss each other, but between school, our jobs, the distance, and our personal lives, we don't have as much time for each other."

He looked at me and asked if I was breaking up with him. "No," I said quickly, "but what I am saying is if this ever becomes too much, then please tell me. I'll understand."

John said, "You're going to be my wife one day, and no distance can stop that."

The phone rang while I was at work. It was my granny. She was crying and said someone had broken into the house while she was at church and taken everything. I asked if she had called the police and if she was OK. She assured me she was fine, but she now had nothing. "I worked so hard for my things," she said. "I can't buy this stuff again."

I cried with her, and for the first time, I realized I didn't have any extra money to help my granny. I was giving her the money Tina gave me, along with paying my tuition. My two jobs covered my bills. I didn't know what to do, but I knew I had to help her. I told her not to worry, that I would ship the things she needed to her. I asked her to give me two weeks. "I'll have everything replaced by then."

"No. You're in school, and you already do enough. I just needed to talk to someone."

"Don't worry," I said. "I'll fix it." I could tell she felt better. "Do you have any idea who did this?" I asked. She was silent for a moment, and I wondered why, and then I thought, *Did my mom do this?* She didn't tell me, but she did say my mom had come to the house earlier to ask for money, and Granny had to tell her no, because she didn't have any extra to give. I was filled with anger, because I had a gut feeling my mom had done this to my granny.

I called Tina and told her I was coming over. I had no other choice anymore. I saw what the girls did night in and night out. I knew I could dance and make good money. When I arrived at Tina's, a guy I'd never seen before was leaving. "Who was that?" I asked Tina.

"A job."

"You do this at home?"

"That guy pays for this home. He's the only person I do this with here and only when the kids are gone." I went inside. "What's up? You seemed like something was wrong when you told me you were coming over."

"I think it's time," I said.

"Time for what?"

"I'll dance. I need the money. Someone broke into my granny's home and took everything, and I have to replace it. She's old and doesn't deserve this, and I must fix it."

Tina looked at me. "OK. We have to get you some clothes and shoes. When do you want to start?"

"As soon as possible. Can you work with me and show me some moves?"

"Yes," she said, "but first, let's go shopping."

We got to the store and picked up enough for at least a full week of dancing with a few changes each night. We went back to Tina's house, and she showed me some moves. We practiced nearly all night. "You're ready," she said. "You're a natural."

"I sure hope so."

Then Tina gasped. "Oh no. We have to give you a name."

"Oh yeah. I didn't think about that."

Tina was silent for a moment. "Whatever it is, it has to be vicious. That's it! Your name is Vicious."

There it was. I had everything I needed now. I just had to put it all together on stage.

On my first night, I felt like a kid going to school for the first time. I was nervous, but I knew what I had to do. With my first performance, I made a few hundred dollars. I was very surprised. It was my first time dancing for money, and oddly enough, I made more money than all the other dancers. Tina was right there watching and protecting me. I felt safe, but I also felt empty. I never thought I would need to dance for money. My first night went very well. After I paid the DJ and my club fee, which Tina gave back to me, I had made $1,300 in four hours.

I was still working my other two jobs, along with dancing four nights a week. I took all my classes on Tuesdays and Thursdays from eight to four. I took these days off from the store and the club so I could study after class before going to FedEx. On Mondays, Wednesdays, and Fridays, I worked all three jobs and ran errands when I could. I was often tired and didn't have time for myself at all anymore. I barely had time to talk to John. We e-mailed and texted a lot. He was understanding, but I could tell it was getting to him. I was making great money—more than enough to take care of my granny and myself. As I had promised, I replaced all my granny's things in two weeks. I was starting to save money as well, because of the cash from the club. Tina was booking me at several private parties that included a fee just for showing up. On average, I was making $3,000 a week.

Christmas break was coming soon, and I planned to go home to Georgia. I hadn't seen my granny or godchild in months. I also missed seeing my dad. The semester was almost over, and my grades were great. I was studying for my last exam in the library when a girl from my business marketing class sat next to me. I thought it was odd, because the library was empty; she could have chosen to sit anywhere. I looked up, and she smiled. "Hi, Rachel."

"Hi," I said. "How do you know my name?"

"We have two classes together, but you always look so mad that I never said anything to you." I looked at her. "But today, since there's no one around, and we're alone, I figured I'd sit next to you and speak. If you're mean to me, then it'll be OK. I won't be embarrassed because there's no one here."

"I see," I said. "I certainly won't be rude! It's nice meeting you."

"You didn't even ask me my name."

"I'm sorry. What's your name?"

"It's Terri with an *i*."

"Nice to meet you, Terri with an *i*." I went back to studying.

She said, "My birthday is tomorrow."

"Great. Happy birthday!" I tried studying again, but I could feel she was still looking at me. "What, Terri with an *i*?"

"What are you getting me for my birthday?"

I laughed. "Nothing. I don't know you."

"Now you do!"

I laughed again. "What do you want for your birthday?"

"Let me think," she said. "I need a new phone for my apartment, glasses, and plates." She laughed. "I'm just joking, but you can call me for my birthday." She gave me her number and left the table.

I thought, *Do I look like I like girls or something?* Terri was pretty. She had long hair and nice teeth, a small frame, and a beautiful smile. *Is she hitting on me, or was she just being nice?* I didn't know, but I figured I would call her on her birthday and pick up the things she mentioned while I was out running errands.

I called her the next day. When she answered, I said, "Happy birthday! This is Rachel."

I could hear the smile in her voice as she said, "Thank you. I didn't think you were going to call."

"What are your plans for today?" I asked.

"I'm hanging out with friends tonight but studying all day for exams."

"Good," I said. "Come to the mall right now. Meet me at Foot Locker." I hung up the phone.

About forty-five minutes later, Terri entered the store. "I didn't know you worked here."

"How would you have known?" I replied. "You're not the kind of girl who wears sneakers!"

She laughed. "You're right." Terri had on a nice fitted dress with heels. She was also wearing an Alpha

Kappa Alpha jacket. I asked if she was an AKA. She laughed. "Yes, silly! Don't you see my jacket?"

I smiled and went to grab her gifts. When I came back out, she was sitting on one of the benches. I handed her the gift bag, and she looked surprised. "What's this?" she asked.

"It's your birthday gift."

She smiled and opened the bag. "Thank you so much, but I was really joking."

"You don't need a phone, glasses, and plates?"

"Yes, I do, but I wasn't expecting you to get them for me!"

From that day forward, Terri and I were connected. We hung out a lot before I left for Christmas break. She knew about all my jobs. Some days, she would stop by the store and bring me food or drop by the club when I was dancing. Tina didn't care much for Terri, and I could tell she was a little jealous. I joked with Tina often and told her she didn't need to worry; she was stuck with me. Tina said, "I just don't trust her. There's something about her that doesn't sit well with me."

7

DEATH FINDS ME

I was finally home and so happy to see my granny. She had aged some while I was away at school, but she was still a beautiful woman. We hung out nearly every day that she was up to it. I was also able to spend a lot of time with Morgan. She had grown up fast. John and I saw each other a few times as well, but we were both busy with our families. John wanted me to come over every day, but I couldn't do that and spend time with my family as well. He spent most of the break upset with me about one thing or another. On Christmas Eve, my goddaughter, Granny, and I went shopping to pick up last-minute gifts. We had a great time laughing and walking, but the mall had taken its toll on my granny. She asked to stop, because she was tired. She kept eating candy. This made me laugh, because my granny always had candy, but she seemed to be eating more than usual. Morgan and I picked up a few more things while my granny rested on the bench. She welcomed us back with a big smile. We headed to the car. We were all tired on the drive home.

I saw that my granny's mouth was filled with vomit. She was choking. I pulled over immediately. She said, "I'm so sorry. I didn't want to mess your car up."

"Don't worry about the car. What's wrong? Are you feeling bad?"

"I ran out of candy," she said. "The candy was stopping me from throwing up. I haven't been able to keep anything in my stomach for a few weeks."

"Have you gone to the doctor?"

"Yes," she said, "a few times, but they keep telling me nothing is wrong."

We were on the side of the road, and it was dark out. It wasn't safe, so we got back in the car after cleaning up with an old shirt I had. I dropped my goddaughter off at home. She was worried about my granny and asked if she was going to be OK. "I sure hope so, sweetie," I said. I told her I loved her and would see her the next day for Christmas. I got back in the car, and my granny and I began to talk. She told me nothing hurt, but she wasn't feeling well. She said she hadn't been able to eat, and when she did, it just came back up. When we got home, my granny took a shower, and then I did the same. By the time I was finished, she was asleep. I decided to get in bed with her that night. I had a strange feeling but didn't know what it was or why, just that I wanted to be close to her as she slept.

On Christmas morning, my granny was up and out of the bed by the time I opened my eyes. She was cleaning as usual. As she was doing that, I took out the gifts I had gotten for my mom. Her drug addiction was even worse than I remembered, and I didn't see or talk to her anymore. I knew she needed shoes, underwear, and clothes. She wasn't working and spent most of her time in the street. She would come home to bathe, or so my granny said.

My granny and I talked and laughed as she opened her gifts. She was looking forward to going to church later that morning, and I was looking forward to seeing Morgan and John. I went to see my goddaughter first. She was up bright and early, as most kids are. Her mother was there. I had not seen Shanae in a while. In fact, I couldn't remember the last time I saw her. It was awkward being near her, and I felt like she was watching me. I focused all my attention on Morgan as she opened her gifts. She was so excited, and it was a great feeling watching her open the presents I had bought for her. After a few hours, I left Morgan with her family and headed to John's house.

When I arrived, John's entire family was at his house: his dad, sister, brother, nieces, and aunts. They were all laughing and eating. It was good to see them. They were a perfect family. John and I ate and laughed with them. We played board games and talked trash while playing cards. There was so much going on that I forgot to give John his present. We went to a room where it was quiet and exchanged gifts. He was happy, and that made me happy. He'd been a little upset with me lately. It seemed to him that I didn't have time for him. My time *was* limited with three jobs and school, but I made time when I could to talk, and I e-mailed and texted him daily.

As John's guests left, he helped them to their cars, while I waited in the house. His father asked me to go out to get wood with him for the fireplace. I said yes, of course. John's father had helped me greatly over the years financially, and he was always very supportive. I respected him a great deal. We talked and laughed as we gathered the wood. He told me how proud of me he was. He mentioned that he wished John was more like me and had his mind made up about what he wanted to do after college. I assured him that John would do very well with whatever he decided to do in life.

When I turned around, John's father was very close to me. I felt very uncomfortable. Before I knew it, he grabbed me and kissed me. I tried to pull away, but he was too strong. I felt like a child being held captive. I heard someone heading to the wood stack, and finally I heard a voice. It was John, and his father let me go. I could hardly believe what had happened. I just stood there listening to John's happy voice asking if we needed help.

"Yes," his father answered quickly. "Come get the wood and take it in." I walked into the house. When John came in, he asked if I was OK.

"Yes," I replied, "but I have to leave." He looked amazed and upset with me. There was no way I could tell him about his father. All I could think about was what might have happened if John had not come when he had. Was all the help John's father had given me just a way to get in my pants? I felt like I had failed John, and I was disgusted with myself. I thought maybe there was something I had done to make John's father feel as if he could kiss me.

Although I enjoyed spending time with my family, I was glad to go back to DC. I didn't see my mother while I was home, but I wasn't surprised. Between my mother and Shanae, I had heard too much negativity from those who reported to me on them. I was now focused, rested, and ready to get back to school and work. I had talked to Terri a few times while I was away, and she asked me to call her when I got home. I also needed to call Tina, but I planned to do that later that night. I thought I would surprise her at the club. I did call Terri, and she asked if I wanted to meet for lunch. I was glad to go. I was getting hungry, and I didn't want to cook.

Terri and I ate and laughed all afternoon. We went back to her place after lunch and watched a movie. It hit me that I had not called Tina. I told Terri I needed to make a phone call so I could let Tina know I was back in town.

Tina was excited to hear from me. "Are you coming to the club?"

"I'm not sure. I want to rest up a little more, but I'll be in tomorrow night for sure."

"OK," she said. "See you later. Love you." I was shocked. She had never told me she loved me before.

"Love you too," I said. "See you tomorrow."

When I hung up, Terri asked, "Who do you love?"

"Oh," I said. "That was a friend, not someone I'm seeing." I sat back down, and we talked. I told her I had a boyfriend whom I cared for deeply back home, and I asked if she was seeing anyone.

"Yes," she said. "I have a boyfriend. He goes to school with us. He's also in one of the classes we take together. I've been with him for a few years, but I'm not happy."

"If you're not happy, then why be with him?"

"I don't know," she said.

We watched TV for another hour. When I realized it was after eight o'clock, I decided to go home and prepare for work instead of going to the club. I told Terri I was heading home and said I'd had a good time hanging out. She took my hand as I was getting up, so I looked back at her. "I don't want you to leave," she said. She leaned in closer to me. "I want you to kiss me. I've wanted that since the first day I saw you in class." I looked at her in silence, and then I kissed her. We kissed, and we touched. She got off the couch and took my hand. We went to her bedroom. She undressed, and when she was done, she took off my clothes. We were both naked, and our body heat connected us differently from before. She was wetter than I had ever felt, and with every touch, she moaned more. Our bodies stayed locked together for hours, and we both came more times than I could count.

When I opened my eyes, it was morning. I had fallen asleep at Terri's place. I sat up and started to get dressed. She looked at me. "Do you have to work?"

"Yes," I said, "but I'll call you later."

I locked the door on my way out and headed to my car. I went home and got ready for work. It seemed that I was in a good place. School was going well, and I was on track to graduate on time. I was still working three jobs, but I wasn't as tired as I used to be. My goal was to finish school and get a good job. I really didn't want to dance, and I was looking forward to ending that chapter of my life, but I was very thankful that I was able to make ends meet.

After work, I went back to Terri's instead of to the club. It was late when my cell rang. I was startled, as I had no idea who would be calling me at this hour. I woke Terri as I picked it up. I feared something was wrong with my granny, but to my surprise, it was my mother. "Your dad was in a very bad accident at work, and he needs you," she said. I was at a loss for words. Finally, I asked her what had happened. "He was working and fell twenty-five feet out of a tree he was cutting down. I'm at the hospital, and they found drugs in his system." I told her I was on my way.

Terri drove down with me to see my dad. I was so rattled that I forgot to call my granny to tell her I was in town but would be staying at a hotel. I had never brought anyone home with me, and I wasn't ready to start now. By now, John and I spoke very little. He was busy with his fraternity, and I was busy with work, school, and Terri.

When I got to my dad's hospital room, I couldn't believe my eyes. The doctors said he was lucky to be alive. The damage was mostly due to the fact that he had landed on both of his feet. If he had landed differently, he would have broken his neck. As it was, he had broken his heel, leg, collarbone, and arm; punctured a lung; and fractured his ribs. The breaks were due to the impact of hitting the ground. I sat next to my dad, and to my surprise, he was crying. I had seen him cry only once before that I remembered.

"You're lucky," I said to my dad. "I'm glad God decided to keep you with me."

He couldn't talk but was able to nod his head. I could tell he was ashamed of what had happened but more so because of why it had happened. My dad had struggled with his addiction for as long as I could remember, and this time, it had nearly cost him his life. I told my dad I was leaving and would see him tomorrow. Terri had stayed at the hotel while I went to the hospital.

As I drove to the hotel, I felt scared for my dad. I called my granny to check on her. She answered on the fourth ring, which was normal for her. "Hi, pretty lady," I said. "How are you?"

"Hey, baby. I'm OK. Your granny is getting old." I asked how she was feeling, but she said she was just OK. That instantly caused tears to run down my face. She didn't sound like herself, and I knew she wasn't feeling well. I told her I would see her tomorrow and explained that I was in town because my dad had had a bad accident.

"I'll be right here if God is willing," she said. I felt so sad at the thought that the two people I cared most about were not doing well. I hoped that whatever was bothering my granny would pass. She never got sick; she was a healthy woman. As for my dad, he was going to heal just fine, but I wasn't sure if he was going to be able to continue his type of work.

When I got to the room, Terri was watching TV. I kissed her and said I was going to shower. She asked if I was OK. I said I wasn't sure. I felt the tears coming, so I went to the bathroom. I undressed and got into the shower. I cried because I was scared and feeling broken. The fear of what could have happened to my dad and the thought of my granny not feeling well for such a long period of time overwhelmed me. I felt Terri's warmth behind me. She held me from behind as I broke down. I had not sobbed in a very long time—since I was in the home after my mother had beaten me. She held me in silence until I pulled myself together. I shut the shower off, turned to her, and whispered, "Thank you." She kissed me, and we held each other for a moment.

We walked to the bed and held each other in silence. It was what I needed. It gave me comfort, and I found enough peace to drift into sleep.

When I opened my eyes, Terri was already awake. She had been watching me sleep. She moved my hand to her wetness. She was ready, and her body was waiting for my touch. We made love and enjoyed the intimate moment as if it were our last. It was intense and different from before.

As we were dressing before leaving to visit my granny, she said, "I love you."

I looked at her, but I had no words. I had gone mute. As I stood there, she grabbed her purse and went to the door. "Are we going, or am I going to have to find my way to your granny's house alone?"

When we arrived at my granny's house, she was in the kitchen washing dishes. "Hey, Granny!" I shouted.

"Hey, baby. I was waiting on you."

I introduced Terri to my granny, and they exchanged pleasantries. My granny wasn't a hugger, and I had warned Terri of this before we arrived. We talked and laughed. Terri and my granny seemed to enjoy each other's company. I was quiet as they talked about school, God, and where Terri was from. My granny was pleased. As we prepared to leave to visit my dad, my granny said to Terri, "You sure are a pretty girl."

We both laughed, and Terri said, "Thank you. You're beautiful too." I hugged my granny, and we said our goodbyes. After visiting my dad, we were getting on the road to head home. I had to work, and I had a private party the next day.

As we were leaving my granny's house, my mother came in. She was so high that she didn't even recognize me. She walked right by me. That was a blow to my heart. Something must have clicked, because she stopped in her tracks and turned around. "Hi, Rachel. I'm so sorry."

I nodded and walked away. For my mother to be so high she didn't recognize her only child was horrible. My granny called for me, and I waved my hand, because I knew she would only make excuses for my mom.

When we got in the car, Terri asked, "Who was that?"

"My mother," I replied. She just stared at me and held my hand. Terri had a good mother, a mother who loved her and was active in her life.

Before I went to the hospital, I stopped to see my godchild. I would never come home and not see her. She was growing fast. As with my last visit, her mother was home. It was more awkward than Christmas. I could tell she was trying to figure out who Terri was. I introduced Terri to Morgan, and they talked awhile. I told Morgan I had to leave but would be back in a few months. I explained that I'd had to come home because my dad had had a bad accident.

We saw my dad, but he was asleep the entire time. The nurse said he was on pain medications that made him very tired. I stayed awhile, and I wrote him a note before I left, letting him know I had visited and would call him the next day from work. As we walked to the car, Terri held my hand. It felt weird, maybe because we were in public, maybe because she had told me she loved me, or maybe because I was just all over the place.

Back at home, work was getting busier with more private parties. By now, I had stopped dancing in the club. I would go only if it was an event or a special request. All my work was private. Tina was seeing a new dude and chick, so she was busy with them. We saw each other a few times a week when I had a party, but we didn't hang out as much anymore. The school year was coming to an end, and I was thankful. I needed a break, but I was taking two classes over the summer so I could graduate in the fall of the upcoming school year.

Terri and I were really serious. She had told her mother about us, but it hadn't gone over well. Her mother had made a lot of threats and did not like the idea of her AKA being with a woman.

I told Terri I understood if she wanted to stop what we were doing, but that made things worse.

"That's not the answer," she said. "I don't expect you to give up because my mother doesn't like it."

I apologized and told her I was so accustomed to people leaving and hurting me that I figured I would give her an easy out and save myself the heartache. I knew I loved her and wanted to be with her, and with that realization, I knew I needed to call John and break things off completely with him. Terri had broken things off with her boyfriend months ago. I guess she didn't worry about John, because he was so many miles away.

She sat next to me and said, "I love you, and I know you love me. You don't have to say it, because you show it every day. No one has ever made love to me the way you do, no one has cared for me the way you do, and no one has ever made sure I had everything I needed every day. I know you love me, and you don't have to say it until you're ready."

I was silent and still.

Things were getting better with my dad, but they were still pretty bad. He had lost his place. I hadn't realized how bad his drug addiction had gotten. He had nowhere to live, and he needed daily assistance with his injuries. There was no one else to care for my dad, so I had no choice but to go home and get him so he could live with me. I was afraid of how that would affect my personal life, but at the same time, I was an adult. I wasn't going to change my life for my dad.

With my dad living with me, we grew closer by the day. He liked and accepted Terri and who she was in my life. John and I spoke very little, but we kept in contact. After I told him about Terri and broke things off, our communication changed drastically. The break was easy and calm, and I wouldn't have expected anything different. I told my dad about everything except the private parties. I figured that was too much for him. But those private parties helped me take care of him financially. He didn't have anything other than his clothes, so I was left to provide for him. Although I was making great money dancing, it was getting harder and harder. I was ready to close that chapter of my life, but I needed the money even more with my dad living with me.

Terri, Dad, and I were having dinner when I got a call. It was my granny. "You need to come get your mother. She's not going to make it out of here, and you need to build a relationship. I'm not going to be here forever, and I don't want you to be alone."

I asked if something had happened to my mother.

She said, "She was out here in these streets, and someone jumped her."

I asked if she was going to be OK.

"Yes," my granny said, "but the next time, someone may kill her."

"What do you want me to do?" I asked my granny.

"I want you to move her up there with you before it's too late. Don't worry. I'll get her there, but I need you to accept her into your home."

I was torn. Both Terri and my dad were looking at me, waiting to see if everything was OK. I could tell my dad was worried. He and my mom had a special bond, and they always forgave each other for their shortcomings. "OK, I will, but I don't know her," I told my granny.

"She's your mother. You'll get to know her better, and she'll get to know you. You two will always be connected."

I felt a heavy burden had been placed on my shoulders. I would now have yet another person to take care of. Both of my parents would be living in my apartment. Both would be trying to get clean from drugs, and both would be without work. I could feel the stress building in my chest.

Terri and I waited at the bus station. Somehow, my granny had gotten my mother on a bus to DC. I couldn't believe it when I got the call telling me my mother would arrive at seven thirty in the morning. Terri was very supportive, but I could tell she was worried. Finally, the bus arrived, and I saw my mother. My stomach dropped. She looked like a ghost and as if she needed to bathe. I could tell she had been crying and needed rest. She looked scary, and if she wasn't my mother, I wouldn't have recognized her.

"Hi," I said, when she approached us.

"Hi, Rachel. Where's your dad?"

"He's home. He isn't able to walk and get around."

She didn't respond, so we walked to the car and headed to the apartment. My two-bedroom apartment was now filled.

It was an adjustment for everyone to get used to living together. I had never lived with both of my parents full-time before. There would be a night here and there but never full-time. Things were changing so fast. Within thirty days, both of my parents were living with me. My dad was healing, and he provided comfort for me when I struggled with my mother. She was having a difficult time being in a place she didn't know, and she was going through withdrawal from the drugs and alcohol. My rule was no drugs or drinking in my home. My mother and I talked very little. She and Terri talked a great deal when Terri was over, but I was spending most nights at Terri's by now.

One evening Terri was in a mood, and I wasn't sure why. I was getting ready to go to the club for a guest performance, and I could tell something was wrong, so I bit the bullet and asked.

"We barely spend time together," she said. "We barely have sex anymore. You work all the time, and you're tired when you get home."

"What do you want me to do?" I asked. "I have to work, and I need each job. Each job provides something the other doesn't. We have to go to school and study as well. I'm doing the best I can."

She started to cry. "I know. I'm sorry. I'm selfish, and I want more of you. I want you to make love to me now. Not later—now."

I kissed her. "Baby, I have to go to work. I'm sorry, but I can't miss this. I've been paid already. Come with

me. I promise we'll make love when I'm done working."
She let out a loud sigh and went to get dressed.

We arrived at the club, and there was barely an
open seat. The party was for KD, and he had a huge
fan base. As I walked in, I spoke to everyone and received hugs from many of the customers and my work
associates. Tina was high on something and very happy
to see me. With all I had going on, we didn't talk much
anymore. We saw each other only when it was time to
make money. She jumped into my arms and kissed me
on my lips. "I love you, and I miss you," she said.

I held her and said, "I love and miss you too!" Terri
was not happy about Tina kissing me or me holding
her. Terri walked away. I told Tina I would catch up
with her. I needed to put Terri in a VIP spot and get
dressed. I walked around the club until I found Terri
talking to her ex-boyfriend. He was surprised to see
me. Not many of the guys on campus came to this club,
and he had no idea I was a dancer. I didn't care that he
knew, but I was concerned about whether it bothered
Terri. I held her hand lightly. I told her I had to get
dressed but wanted to show her where she would be sitting. She looked at me, and I knew she was upset. She
said goodbye to her ex-boyfriend and came with me. I
took her to her seat in the VIP area, but when I went to
hug her, she pulled away. I didn't make a fuss, because
I needed to get dressed. It was going to be a big night.

As I walked to the dressing room, a woman who often attended the parties that Tina booked me for was

smiling at me. I greeted her, because she was one of my best customers. I was nervous that she would want to hug, because Terri was already upset with me. As I got closer to my client, she kissed me on the cheek and hugged me tightly. I returned the favor and hugged her as well. This was my job, and Terri knew that.

The night went by quickly. I had a great performance, and a lot of money followed the show. When I was done, I got dressed and went to Terri. I asked if she was OK. She had been drinking, and I could tell she was more relaxed. "Yes, I'm OK," she said. "You did well. Can we leave now?"

"Yes, let's go get my bag." I took her hand, and we headed to the dressing room. When I opened the door, there were a few young women in the corner of the room having sex. A few were getting high, and some were drinking and talking loudly. I grabbed my things, and as I was walking out, one of the girls said, "Vicious, can I eat your pussy?" I didn't respond but kept moving so Terri and I could get out of there. I left without telling Tina, because I knew Terri was close to killing me by now.

We got in the car, and Terri didn't say one word. When we got to her place, she got out of the car without waiting for me. I grabbed my bag and walked in behind her. When I got in, she started yelling. "Are you sleeping with the dancers? Do you participate in the sex? Are you sleeping with Tina? Who was that woman you hugged? Are you sleeping with your male customers?"

The questions were coming fast, and I replied as quickly as I could. The answer was no to everything. I told her I was sorry she was upset. I tried to hold her, but she pulled away. She asked me to leave. I stood there in disbelief. "Are you serious?" I asked.

"Yes," she replied. "I want you to leave." I grabbed my keys and drove home. When I arrived at my apartment, I texted her and told her I was sorry.

The next day, I finally saw Terri's ex-boyfriend in class. She had mentioned we all had a class together, but I hadn't noticed until today. I got to class before Terri. When she arrived, she sat with her ex. This made me upset, but I didn't say anything. After class, I asked her if I could talk to her, and she nodded. "Why are you doing this?" I asked.

"Doing what?" she said. "You don't have time for me, and you're probably sleeping with your customers from the club."

I looked at her. "Terri, I am not, and I would not."

We stood there for a second, and then she turned and walked away. My shoulders felt heavy, and I was hurt that she would think I was sleeping with my customers. I called her when I got home, but she didn't answer. Both of my parents asked me where she was. She was normally with me when I went home. I told them we weren't talking, and neither said anything. I took Terri's lack of communication as confirmation that we were over.

I was working at the store when a woman came in with her friend. I could tell they were older and not in school. I went over to help them, and they were both laughing. One of them said, "My friend Tia walks by this store at least twice a week, and she wants to know if you're seeing someone and if you're interested in females."

I laughed. "Shouldn't Tia be asking me if I'm interested in girls?"

The friend said, "Exactly!"

I could tell Tia was embarrassed her friend had outed her. I smiled and said, "Hi, Tia. Yes, I like girls. It's nice to meet you. My name is Rachel."

Tia finally spoke. "I'm sorry about my friend; she's crazy. I've seen you for the last few months, and I'd like to give you my number so you can call me sometime."

I smiled and said, "Sure." I also gave her my number and told her to feel free to give me a call.

As I was giving Tia my number, Terri walked in. I knew this was going to be bad. Terri walked up to us. "Who is this, and what are you giving her?"

"Hi, Terri," I said. "This is Tia." Terri didn't respond. She turned her back to Tia and faced me. Tia took my number and left the store.

Again Terri asked, "Who was that?"

"A customer was interested in having my number, so I gave it to her, and I took hers."

"Why?" Terri said.

I looked at her and laughed as I walked behind the counter. "What am I supposed to do? You're not taking my calls, and I know you've been hanging out with your ex-boyfriend." Terri looked at me in surprise. "Yes, I know you're hanging out with him." I asked her to leave my store. If she wanted to talk, then we could when I got off.

Things were crazy with Terri, and it was time to call it quits. I had a little more time, and I spent it with my parents. We were all starting to enjoy one another as a family. It was a good feeling, but it was still very hard for me to forgive my mom for all she had done to me and all she had missed in my life. Although we had bad days, we also had good days.

One day, the house phone rang, and my mom answered. I could tell it was bad news. My mom said, "Where is she now? I'll call you back. Thank you so much." When my mom hung up, she said, "My mother fell." My mom called the house, and my aunt picked up. My mom said, "Where is Mama? Is she OK? What happened?" I was nervous and scared. My stomach started to hurt, because I knew it was bad news. I heard my mom say, "I'm coming home, but you need to take her to the ER." After my mom hung up with my aunt, I asked what had happened to my granny. "She fell and is too weak to walk. She needs to go to the ER, and your aunt said she can't take her, because she has to go to work." I started to cry. There was nothing I could do in DC; my granny was in Georgia. My mom made another call, and I heard her say, "Please go to my mother's house and take her to the ER. She needs help, and I'm in Washington, DC." After a pause, she said, "Thank you. Thank you so much."

When my mom hung up, I said, "Auntie wouldn't take Granny?" My mom shook her head. "Then who did you call to take her?"

My mom said, "A friend who I used to get high with in the streets. I know she'll make sure she gets there." My mother and I both went to our rooms to pack our bags. My dad still wasn't able to travel, so we left him and headed to Georgia to be with my granny. I knew it was something bad. For the last few months, she had not been feeling well. I could feel my soul shift and start to break into pieces.

When we arrived at the hospital, they told us my granny had to stay, because they had tests to run. Granny was in a room, wide-awake and watching TV. When she saw me, she smiled and said, "Hey, baby. You got here fast." I smiled and asked how she was feeling. My granny simply smiled without words. I told her she had to stay for some tests, but she already knew.

After we waited for hours, the doctor finally came in with the test results. My heart was pounding. The doctor said, "Mrs. Reynolds, is it OK for me to speak with your guests in the room?"

Granny nodded.

"You have stage four stomach cancer," the doctor said. "We're sorry, but there's nothing that can be done. This is a fast-growing cancer, and we expect you'll live another ten weeks with this illness."

My heart dropped. The room was spinning, and my tears were flowing. I heard my mother sobbing.

The doctor said, "I'll give you time with your family."

After he left the room, I looked at my granny.

She said, "I guess there's nothing they can do to help me. We all have to leave this place, baby."

"I'm not ready to lose you," I said. "We need more time. Granny, I graduate from college in two months, and you have to be there." She smiled, but I couldn't find one to return to her. I lay in the bed next to my granny, feeling as though my heart and soul were being chipped away.

My mom started calling our family and the church. Within thirty minutes, the room was filled with people. I lay there in silence as everyone talked. I decided to get up and take a walk. I went down to the lobby, and as the elevator door opened, I saw Shanae sitting at the reception desk. She had not changed much from high school; she was still thin. I did notice that she had cut her hair, and it fit her well. She looked like a model. I was surprised to see her, and I really didn't want to talk. We made eye contact as I stepped out of the elevator. "Are you here visiting a friend?" she asked.

I said, "No, my granny is here. She's been here for two days now, and more than likely, she's not going home." When Shanae asked what was wrong, I told her and then started to cry immediately. She came from behind the desk and held me. I pulled myself together and thanked her. I told her I was going for a walk.

I traveled back and forth to Georgia every weekend. I would leave on Thursday after class and return on Sunday. Terri called daily to check on my granny and me. Tia and I were seeing each other. I would get a few calls a week from people checking on my granny. I even spoke to John a few times. My mother never came back to DC. She stayed at the hospital with my granny around the clock. I wasn't working nearly as much, because I was driving to Georgia every Thursday. I had money saved, and I wasn't worried about my finances. My body and mind were tired. My granny was dying, and with each passing week, her health deteriorated. I saw Shanae every week at the hospital, and she offered to let me stay in her apartment when I was in town, because it was near the hospital. I showered there each day but slept at the hospital with my granny. Shanae and I talked very little, but we were still connected, and we didn't need any words. When we did speak, it was about my granny.

People were in and out of my granny's room all day. My granny never complained about pain, and she refused all pain medications. She said only God could help her now. She praised God daily, and the praise was loud when the pain came. She was faithful to God and his promise. Her strength was amazing with all that was going on around her. With the exception of my mother, her children argued and came to the hospital drunk. My granny didn't drink, so I thought it was very disrespectful of them to come to the hospital drunk when she was dying.

One of my aunts wanted my granny's life-insurance policies. She was worried about the money. My granny didn't answer her. She had told me where the insurance policies were a few weeks ago, because she didn't trust her kids to bury her with the insurance money. I kept this to myself and endured the questions with her.

One Sunday, when it was time for me to head back to DC for school and work, I asked my granny if she needed anything. "No, baby," she said, and she reached for my hand. "You're destined to do great things, and I know you'll do well. I love you, and I'm proud of you. You were always special, and I knew you would be something one day. I'm not going to make it to your graduation."

That was a blow to my heart. I'd thought she would get better somehow. I'd thought God would fix it, but he hadn't. I listened in silence as she spoke, and I cried tears of hurt and loss. Cancer was defeating us, and our time was coming to an end.

I had been back in DC for two days when my mother called.

"You should come home today. The doctors said Mama may not make it through the weekend."

I dropped everything and drove to Georgia. I didn't want my granny to pass away without me there. I drove close to a hundred miles per hour the entire way. When I arrived, my granny was in a deep sleep. They had given her pain medication to keep her comfortable, as the pain had grown to be unbearable.

I immediately went to her to tell her I was there. I hoped she could hear me. For the first time I thought to myself of how far my granny and me had come. How at one time she was so mean and my early memories of her taking me to the Laundromat. I never asked her about those times. That night was long and dreadful. She got worse as the night went on, and at 2:11 a.m., my granny passed away. She had gone to heaven.

8

SLEEPLESS NIGHTS

The days and nights ran together, and sleep eluded me. I was lost in grief and sadness. I had been in bed for days without eating. I didn't want to see daylight or anyone's face. The thought of seeing my granny in that casket haunted me every minute of every hour. Seeing her body bagged and taken away played in my head over and over. I had taken time off from all my jobs. I needed more time to heal and to cope with losing her. It felt like I needed a miracle to help me get up and continue my life. I was lost and broken. This time, it wasn't because of being abused and neglected by my mother, because of lost friendships or relationships, or because of finances. It was the one thing that couldn't be fixed or replaced: I had lost my granny, and our days together in this life were long gone.

The people in attendance at her funeral were all a blur. I received many calls, which my mom and dad did their best to deflect, because they knew I didn't want to talk to or see anyone. Terri had come by a few times, and she sat with me in silence. Terri and John both attended my Granny's funeral, but I noticed that Shanae didn't come. I should not have been surprised, but deep down, I was hurt that she hadn't shown. Tia decided not to come, and that led to the end of our relationship. I no longer had room for her in my grief and sadness. I was trapped inside myself and couldn't find a way out.

The days and nights were still long, but I had managed to go back to work and to complete my finals. Graduation was days away, and I couldn't imagine walking across that stage without my granny there. So I decided not to walk. I thought it was pointless anyway. I was still grieving, and although the pain had not eased, I was able to mask it when I was on campus. I was starting to lose interest in everything, and I didn't know how to pick up the pieces.

I had decided not to dance any longer. I was tired, and I had enough money saved to be OK until I got a job after graduation. One evening, after a long dreadful day at Foot Locker and FedEx, I was reading in my room when my mom came in. "You've had many phone calls, and I know you don't want to talk," she said. "But you've gotten a call for the last four days from the same company wanting to interview you for a job. I've made an excuse each time, and finally, I told them you had lost your grandmother and were grieving. I didn't want you to miss this opportunity, so I set an appointment for you to have a phone interview tomorrow morning at eight."

I looked at her blankly. "OK," I replied. I hadn't even been thinking about jobs after college, but I knew it was time to start.

The phone rang at eight o'clock on the dot the next morning. I answered, and the woman on the other end said she was calling from Johnson & Johnson. The interview lasted for approximately twenty minutes. I felt it went well. I was ready from all the work I had done all year preparing for interviews. At the end of the interview, the woman told me if I made it to the second round, then I would receive a call the next day to set a time for the second interview. I thanked her for her time and disconnected.

My mom and dad stood in the doorway of my room for the entire interview. I told them I thought it had gone well. They both smiled, and my dad said, "Rachel, I know you're still grieving over your grandmother, but it would mean the world to me if I could see you walk across that stage. You deserve to walk. You've worked hard. You're graduating with honors. You earned that degree while working multiple jobs. You deserve to walk, and I really would like to see you do it." I looked at him and agreed.

The following morning, I ate breakfast with my dad before heading to work. My mom answered the phone when it rang and then handed it to me with a big smile. It was Johnson & Johnson calling to schedule a second interview. I accepted proudly, and for the first time since my granny passed, I felt happy.

"I'm flying to Los Angeles tomorrow morning for my second interview," I told my parents. "I'll be there for three days to complete the interview process."

My parents were filled with joy, and so was I. I felt good about my chances of being hired, and I knew it was a great opportunity for me.

LA was amazing. I enjoyed every second of it, and I knew I could live there if I got the job. The interview process was long and intense. Each day, I had a series of interviews with different department managers. Although the interviews were grueling, everyone was very nice and accommodating. Each night I was there, I went to dinner with the staff, and I got to see the city. Something was planned for me to do each night.

When I got back home, I began to mentally prepare for graduation, which was two days away. My parents were very excited, and although I was excited too, I was also very sad my granny wasn't going to be there. That was a tough pill to swallow, but I knew she would have wanted me to walk that stage. So I did just that.

On the morning of graduation, I dressed and got ready to head to the arena where the ceremony was being held. The phone rang as I was leaving, and I answered it. It was Johnson & Johnson extending an official job offer to me, with a formal declaration by mail to follow. I smiled big and was thankful. I knew my granny was watching over me, and I was sure she'd had something to do with my getting this job. I was told there had been more than one thousand candidates, and only fifty had been selected.

When I disconnected, I yelled to my parents, "I got the job!" They ran out of their room, and for the first time, we all hugged as a family.

Graduation was long and boring, but nonetheless it was a moment of triumph. I had made it. I was the first person in my family to graduate from college. I was ready to see my parents and ready to eat. My dad hugged me and said, "Job well done. I'm so proud of you." My mom also hugged and congratulated me. We left for a celebratory lunch. On our way to the car, I saw Terri and her family, and we stopped to congratulate each other. We kept it brief, as we were both celebrating with our families.

9

NEW BEGINNINGS

I adjusted well to my new career and city. I learned that I could live anywhere in the world, because without my granny, I had no true attachments to a city—or to anything else, for that matter. The only reason I visited Georgia was to see my godchild. I was enjoying LA and all that came with it. I buried myself in my work, the gym, and partying with the new people I had met at work and in the city. I found a circle of friends in no time, and the party life was all that seemed to matter to everyone. I joined in and found my place.

I was dating several people but no one I took a real interest in. I had decided I would have fun and stay away from commitments. My past relationships hadn't seemed to last for one reason or another. My heart had grown cold, and love was a feeling I wanted to avoid altogether. I kept in contact with both Tia and Terri, but we were just friends. The one thing I did love was my job. My work habits and performance stood out. I received a promotion within the first six months, and things were looking good for future promotions within the company.

Work had become more demanding with my new promotion, and I was traveling a great deal from state to state and coast to coast. I was the lead assistant to the company's marketing manager, and he kept me busy. I reported to him and his staff weekly on my research in the field. While traveling, I worked with different small companies that purchased from our company. My job was to help them increase their sales, and in return, they would purchase more of our products. I was a natural at selling and building relationships. This was surprising, given the lack of trust in my personal life, but work was my safe haven. I went from working three jobs as an undergraduate to working one job that I loved.

I was able to see my parents and Morgan while traveling for business. I planned a trip to the East Coast once a month, alternating between DC and Georgia. Morgan was growing up, and she was interested in sports as well as music. I was very happy to be able to see her play in a few games. As for my parents, they were both working and doing better as a couple than ever before. They had made DC their home and had found a new, healthier life without drugs.

I was promoted again, to merchandising and marketing director. I had been with the company for two years, and life was good. My closet was now filled with designer shoes, dresses, and business suits. As I made more money, it went into my closet for work. I was seeing a beautiful young woman named Sharon, and we had been dating for more than six months when we decided to be exclusive. She often stopped people in their tracks when she entered a room. She was very quiet but fun. She was a lawyer for the company. I enjoyed being with her, but there was something about her that was hidden. She was the first person I had talked to about my granny. We often traveled together for business, and with both of our busy schedules, work allowed us to see each other, because we were able to schedule trips to the same cities.

Sharon and I discussed our plans for the upcoming Christmas and New Year's holidays. We were going to be with our families, so we would be separated from each other. We decided to celebrate Christmas early and agreed to bring in the New Year when we both returned to LA. We planned a short trip to Toronto for a few days. We were lucky, because we both had three weeks off. We would spend the first week in Toronto, the second week with our families, and the third together. I was going to Georgia, and she was going to Hawaii, where she was from.

Canada was freezing at that time of year but beautiful. Neither of us had been to Toronto, and we were excited to be together. We stayed in our room the first two nights, making love from sunup to sundown. We came up for air to eat and shower. Because we both wanted to excel in our careers, we normally felt rushed with everything we did, but this was different, because we had been able to leave our laptops at home. We decided to tour the city on the third day and see what Toronto had to offer. Sharon was excited about going to different restaurants, and I just wanted to see the culture. We spent all day sightseeing. When we got back to the hotel, we showered and dressed for dinner. We decided to eat at a highly recommended restaurant, which meant we had to dress up. I wore a black fitted dress with red heels, and ironically, Sharon wore a red dress with black heels. We each laughed when we saw what the other was wearing. As we finished our makeup, we talked about our day.

Dinner was amazing. We decided to go dancing at a local club afterward. Sharon had a few glasses of wine, and we danced all night. As we were leaving, several guys tried to convince us to go back to their hotel for more fun. We politely declined their offer. As Sharon helped me put on my coat, she turned me around; held my face in her hands; kissed me softly; and said, "I love you." I was silent as I looked into her eyes without words. She smiled and said, "Let's go. I'm ready to get you into bed."

When we awoke, it was afternoon. Sharon and I were both exhausted from a long day of touring and a long night of dancing and making love. We decided we would go to the CN Tower and Ripley's Aquarium. I was dressed before Sharon and patiently waited for her. I had a strange feeling that I was trying to place. I couldn't stop thinking about those three words: *I love you*. My relationships with the last three people who had said them hadn't turned out well, and I wished she had not said them. Things seemed to go badly after those words were spoken. I was also wondering how she felt, because I hadn't said the words back. I wondered if I'd hurt her feelings, but I wasn't going to ask. The truth was that I didn't want to talk about it at all. Sharon was finally ready, and we left to have another great day of adventure. I had decided I was going to have a great time and put those thoughts out of my mind for the time being.

We had a wonderful time in Canada. We were headed back to LA so we could prepare to see our families for the holiday. As our Uber drove up, Sharon said, "You don't love me."

I stopped in my tracks and turned to look at her. She had a straight face, but she was a lawyer and could be hard to read. I hadn't been able to tell the day before whether she was bothered by my lack of response, but now I knew she was. Again, I was at a loss for words and just stared at her. She got into the car. I felt like an idiot and hoped I hadn't ruined things for us. I got into the car, and we drove to the airport in silence. We didn't speak on the flight back to LA either, and I felt like I had ruined our trip. We had driven together in my car to the airport, but Sharon told me once we got our luggage that she would take an Uber home. I didn't fight with her, because I knew she had made her mind up. She walked away from me without saying goodbye, which hurt my feelings, but I supposed her feelings had been hurt the last few days, so I deserved what I got.

When I arrived in Atlanta, I was looking forward to seeing my family. I still hadn't spoken to Sharon. I had called a few times, but she didn't answer. I figured we were over, as I had not seen or talked to her in days. I focused my attention on my family and mentally ended my relationship with Sharon. I decided to visit Morgan, and to my surprise, her entire family was there. They were playing cards and eating. Morgan asked me to stay, and I said yes. I had not played cards in a long time, and I had forgotten how much I enjoyed it. Shanae was there, but I didn't feel awkward this time for some reason. I could tell something was different about her, and for the first time in years, when we were in the same room, it felt like we were friends again—that we hadn't missed a day since high school. After playing cards, we sat in the living room and talked for hours. We caught up on the last few years. She had gone back to college and graduated. She was working a steady job but looking for something better. She had a new house and was no longer living in the small apartment. That was great news, because my goddaughter had a larger room to decorate. When I realized the time, I told her I needed to go. I hadn't booked a hotel, and it was late. Shanae looked at me and said I could stay at her place if I wanted to. I didn't know what to say. It was nice of her to offer, but I was unsure. Before I could respond, my goddaughter said, "Yes, stay with us, and you can sleep with me!" I couldn't refuse her, so I agreed.

When I got out of the shower, Morgan was sound asleep. I saw Shanae on her bed, reading. I asked her what she was reading, and she said, "*Between Lovers.*" I had not read the book, but I knew the author.

"You still don't sleep at night, do you?"

She smiled and said, "No."

I told her to enjoy her book and wished her good night. As I was walking to my goddaughter's room, Shanae asked, "Why did you leave me here? It was hard without you. I needed you."

I stopped and looked at her. "It was time for me to move on. You had changed, and my heart was broken." I walked to Morgan's room. I tossed and turned, and finally, I decided to sleep on the couch, because I didn't want to wake Morgan. I found a blanket on a chair in her room, and I took the pillow I had. It was dark, and I was unfamiliar with the house, but it was cozy and small, and my memory led me to the couch. When I went to sit down, I sat on Shanae's legs. I was startled, and Shanae said, "It's just me."

"I'm sorry," I said. "I thought you were in your bed."

"I don't sleep in my bed much. I normally fall asleep on the couch." I apologized again and had started to head back to the room when she stopped me. "You can sleep in my bed if you want. I'm going to stay out here."

I stopped, turned around, and headed back to the couch. I asked if it was OK for me to sit with her, and she said yes. We talked. She told me more about our time apart and her life, and I told her about mine. We both had had a few relationships. She had only been with men, and after John, I had only been with women. She told me an ex-boyfriend had raped her, which was hard to hear. She started to cry, and my natural instinct was to hold her, so that's what I did. She'd had a pretty bad set of relationships—and I thought things were jacked up for me. We eventually fell asleep, and when morning came, we were in the same positions in which we had fallen asleep. For a moment, it felt like no time had passed by between us, though it had been at least eight years.

I went to see my mom's side of the family. Everyone was laughing and talking. It was early in the day, and my mom was already drunk. I had gotten accustomed to her not drinking anymore. She was loud and aggressive, a feeling I remembered all too well. Suddenly, it all rushed back to me like an ocean wave. I was back in that place where she was beating me into shock, that place where I was stuck inside myself and wanted to die. I had not thought about that day or felt this way in a long time, and it made me mad. All I wanted to do was yell and scream at her for being drunk.

Instead, I left to visit my dad's side of the family. When I got there, they said my dad had left, but no one knew where he was. I had a bad feeling. He would have called if he was going to leave, because he knew I was coming to see him and his family. I stayed awhile and enjoyed my family, all the while praying my dad wasn't doing what I thought he was.

Shanae had given me a key, so I went back to her house. She told me she would be at her family's house all day, so I wasn't surprised that no one was there. I grabbed a pillow and went to the couch to take a nap. The memories that had come up had made me angry, sad, mad, and even scared. I was an adult now, and my life was good. I couldn't understand why I was scared. When I opened my eyes, Shanae was watching me. "How long have you been home?" I asked.

"A few hours," she said.

"What time is it?"

"Nine," she said.

I couldn't believe I'd slept that long, and I wondered how long she'd watched me sleep. "How was your day?"

I told her what had happened. We sat on the couch again and talked for hours, laughing about the good times we'd shared in high school. We'd had a lot of good days, and they overshadowed the few bad ones.

It was getting late, and I announced that I was going to bed. Shanae took my hand, and I could instantly feel the connection between us. She stood behind me and held me close to her body. I could feel her body heat and her heartbeat. She hugged me and said, "I've missed you." In that moment, I realized I had missed her too, and the connection we'd shared had not gone away. We walked to her bedroom, and I sat her down. I took her clothes off and then removed my own. Our bodies connected as we felt each other's wetness. We kissed and touched each other. I could feel her growing close to orgasm and knew it was going to be intense. I felt her arms tighten around me and her legs begin to tremble. She let out a loud gasp, and I felt tears falling from her eyes as she fought against her orgasm. I held her close as her entire body shook. When she had calmed, I kissed her tears as she drifted to sleep.

Everyone was excited on Christmas Eve as they prepared for the next day. I still had not heard from my dad, and I couldn't stand the sight of my mom. I was ready to get back to work. I was confused about the feelings welling inside me for Shanae; I was worried that my dad had disappeared; and I was angry about my mom's drunken episode, which made me want to stay far away from her. On the bright side, my god-daughter was happy and excited. I slept with her that night, because I wanted to see her face when she awoke on Christmas morning. The next day, all I heard was her feet running to the tree to open presents. She was so excited. As she opened her gifts, her mother and I watched, smiling at her joy. Shanae and I didn't talk about our sexual encounter, and I thought maybe it had been a mistake. I knew we had things we needed to discuss, but neither of us was ready to face those truths, so we didn't. We left things in a silent place. A few days later, I went back to my life in LA.

I still had not heard from my dad, and I knew he'd had a relapse. It seemed that both my parents were back to their addictions. I thought they had done so well, but maybe not. I was living in LA, and they clearly had told me the story they wanted me to hear. Nonetheless, I was happy to be home and looked forward to going back to work. I decided to work the last week of my vacation. I no longer had plans with Sharon, and I didn't want to sit around my place for an entire week when I could be getting things done. Most of my coworkers were off, so I was in the office by myself. I was able to work on a project that could lead to my next promotion, and I was excited about my progress. At the rate I was working, I would have a new account as well as the company's largest account closed by the time my boss returned from vacation.

10

MOVING FORWARD

I had been promoted a few months ago, which meant another move. Moving never bothered me, and when there was an opportunity for me on the East Coast, I was ready. I lived in New York now, and the city moved at a much faster pace than LA—and definitely faster than Georgia. It reminded me of a slower and smaller DC. The city lights were always shining brightly, and the city never slept. The view from my condo was amazing. I could see the entire city.

I was looking forward to my first day in my new office with my new colleagues. In my normal fashion, I wore a fitted black dress and black heels. Many smiling faces greeted me, and my new team was eager to get to work. During my travel in my previous job, I'd had the opportunity to meet most of the staff in the New York office, so I was very familiar with the building and my colleagues. We jumped right in and got to work. I was looking forward to bringing magic to my new city and my company.

It was nice being closer to my parents, but they were both in a bad place. My dad was back on drugs, and although my mother was not, she was drinking heavily. I often received calls from my mom about my dad not paying the rent or not coming home for days. These conversations made me upset, because she expected so much from my dad but had given me so little as a young child and teenager. Shanae and I saw each other a few times, and she had come to LA, but by the time I was promoted to the New York office, we were no longer seeing each other. I still hadn't gotten over what she had done to me in high school. We tried to maintain a friendship, but it was too hard. The one thing I learned in the process was that I loved her; that hadn't seemed to change over the years. Word on the street was that Shanae was seeing someone, and that someone was a woman. Other than with me and now with this new woman, Shanae had only been in relationships with men. I wasn't sure how I felt about that, but I wanted her to be happy. I knew I didn't want to be in a relationship with her. Although our bond was stronger than I cared to admit, I didn't trust her. To be honest, it scared me, and it was easier to run from it.

I found a group of friends to hang out with in New York, and we spent most weekends partying. I loved being able to attend plays and go to local clubs to listen to live jazz music. Although my social life was great, my love life was nonexistent, but that didn't last for long. I went out one night to a local jazz club with one of my friends, who had arranged for a few people to meet us there. When her group of friends arrived, we got a table and ordered drinks. One young woman in particular seemed to be watching me the entire night. The musicians were amazing, and we enjoyed a lot of great conversation and laughter. I didn't feed into the energy, because I was drained from my previous relationships. I was enjoying being single and not dating. I had more time for my work and the gym, but at the end of the night, she asked for my number and wanted to know if I'd like to hang out sometime. I was perplexed initially but thought maybe she just wanted to be friends. I gave her my number and headed to my Uber. When I got to the car, I realized I hadn't asked her name.

On Saturday morning, I was looking forward to working out with my trainer, whom I saw three times a week. My phone rang on my way to the gym. It was the girl from the night before. Her name was Joan. "Do you have plans tonight?" she asked and invited me to another local jazz club I had not been to. I told her I would meet her there at eight, and we disconnected.

I was running late to the club and didn't arrive until a little after nine. I hadn't been sure what I wanted to wear, and I'd changed clothes three times. I finally decided to wear a pair of jeans with a black bodysuit and black heels. Blue jeans with a black top and heels always worked. When I walked in, I could see Joan sitting at a table with her drink. I walked over and apologized for being late.

She smiled. "That's OK. I'm glad you made it out."

Our other friends were not there, so I knew my first thoughts about Joan's intentions were wrong. I sat down, and she asked what I was drinking. I declined, and we began to talk. Joan was very nice. She was a freelance photographer between jobs. She was born and raised in the Bronx. She was a Puerto Rican with a very mild attitude and personality. We had a great conversation, and Joan made it clear she wanted to take me out on a date. She had long, silky hair, and her skin was like coffee with cream. At the end of the night, I agreed to see Joan again. I told her to call me, and we would set a date.

I still traveled a great deal for work and was packing my bag for a business trip when Joan called to ask if I wanted to get something to eat. I had to decline, as I was due at the airport in the next few hours. Joan and I had been talking often on the phone and seeing each other at least once a week. She was easy to talk to, and she never gave me a hard time about work and my travel. That was a great feeling, because work was very demanding, and I was often pulled in many directions. Before hanging up, I told Joan we would get together when I returned. I offered her the choice of hanging out at my condo. Joan had never been to my place; normally, we went out. Joan lived with a friend, and I knew I would never hang out there.

After my trip, Joan came to my apartment, and I cooked dinner. Afterward, we sat on the couch and watched a movie. When it ended, Joan and I talked about her work and the lack of jobs. I was positive and told her to keep searching, that she would find something soon. Joan had gotten quiet, and I asked if something was wrong. She was silent for a moment. Then she said, "Kiss me."

I had been down this road before, and before I did anything, I said, "I'm not looking for a relationship right now, and I don't want to ruin our friendship. I've not had successful relationships for one reason or another, and it likely has been my fault, not the other person's. I have trust issues, and in some ways, I've grown cold. My childhood wasn't great, and I struggle with being able to fully love."

She listened patiently and then took my hand. "Kiss me," she said again. I leaned in and kissed her.

Night had become morning, and I got up to cook breakfast for Joan. She was sleeping peacefully, and I didn't want to wake her. I left a note on the table with her food. I headed to my office to work on a few things before an upcoming trip the following day. When I arrived at the office, the building was empty and quiet, just the way I liked it. I got more work done when there was no one coming into my office to talk to me. I wrapped up the things I needed to complete and headed back to my place. On my way out the door, Joan called to thank me. I told her I was heading back, and she apologized for sleeping so late. I told her it was OK and said I would see her soon.

Things between Joan and me became serious, and she was on hard times. She was going from place to place, and jobs were still few and far between. We had been dating for more than a year at that point. I was traveling most of the month with a new project I was working on, so I asked Joan if she wanted to move in.

She said, "I can't move in. I can't afford to help you with this place. I don't make enough money in six months to pay the rent here one month." I told her not to worry about the money and said I would cover all the bills. She agreed and moved in. It was great. Joan cleaned and always had my things nice and organized. She was always there to help me with whatever I needed. I remained positive when she spoke about work, but I was starting to think she needed to look at something else besides freelance photography. The conversation didn't go as well as I'd hoped, but she was receptive.

Joan began working for a local art gallery. The money wasn't great, but it was a step in the right direction. She often complained about her work and pay. I was starting to tire of her lack of effort and drive, so I stopped giving my opinion. I was out of the city even more for a project in my hometown. Being able to see Morgan made my home situation better. I saw Shanae at times, but she was in a relationship, and we both agreed not to spend time alone. Joan had started to gain weight, and with each passing day, she was growing unhappier with herself. She spent many days locked in the room and not talking at all. On these days, I would prepare her food and stay out of the way.

Joan decided she wanted to travel down south with me, because I was going to be there a full week working. She also wanted to meet my goddaughter. I thought it was a great idea, so I agreed. She was having a good week, so I figured we would build on that. I made plans to have dinner with Morgan and Joan the first night. When we arrived at Shanae's apartment, my goddaughter wasn't ready yet. She'd had practice after school and was getting changed. Shanae invited me to sit and wait, and I told her I had a friend with me. She gave me a complex look as I headed to the car to get Joan. I introduced them, but they had little to say to each other. Joan knew of Shanae and a little about our past, but Shanae didn't know about Joan. When she and I spoke, it was about Morgan, and that was it. We weren't really friends, more like coparents. Finally, Morgan was dressed and ready to go. Shanae was home alone, so I asked if she'd had dinner. She said she would grab something after we left. I felt horrible, so I invited Shanae to dinner with us. I could see that made Morgan happy, but not Joan. Shanae agreed to join us, and we all headed out.

We arrived at the restaurant, and I sat between my goddaughter and Joan. Shanae sat across from me. We ate and talked. Joan and Morgan got along well and had a few things in common. Shanae was quiet during dinner, but we had an awkward energy even without words—an energy that I felt was obvious to everyone at the table. We made eye contact many times and were both conscious of breaking that contact. Joan asked why I was so quiet, but I told her I was having fun listening to her and Morgan talk. We wrapped up dinner and went to the car. The drive home was quiet; Morgan had fallen asleep. As I was driving, I could feel Shanae looking at me, and every so often, when I looked in my rearview mirror, our eyes met. When we pulled up to her apartment, I got out to walk them in. My goddaughter and I said our goodbyes. Shanae said, "Meet me in thirty minutes at our spot." I didn't have to ask what spot, because I knew. In high school, Shanae and I would go to a park not too far from where we grew up, but I didn't know why she wanted to meet. I just said OK.

My hotel wasn't far from the park. I had to tell Joan something about why I was leaving so soon after getting back. I parked at the door, planning to walk Joan upstairs and to use the restroom. As we walked into the hotel, Joan asked why I had parked by the door, and I told her I was going back out briefly. She looked puzzled and said, "You're going to meet Shanae, aren't you?"

"Yes," I replied. Normally, Joan wasn't so forward, so I was surprised at her question. "She wants to talk."

Joan chuckled and said, "I bet."

I asked, "What's that supposed to mean?"

"You two were looking at each other all night at dinner. I figured she would want you to herself."

"It's not like that," I said. "We haven't shared a romantic relationship in years." Joan got in the elevator without responding.

I pulled up to the park, and Shanae was already there. She got out of her car and into the back seat of mine. I joined her and locked the door. As I was about to ask what was wrong, Shanae got on my lap and started taking her shirt off. We embraced and kissed. Her body was hot, and I could feel the heat as our bodies connected. For the first time, we made love in the back seat of a car. Each moment was intense, and her wetness was even more than I remembered. When she was close to orgasm, she tried to pull away, but I held her tight and finally, her body exploded. She yelled out and then buried her face in my neck. Soon after, she began to dress, and I did the same. "My partner is home, and I know she's going to have questions."

I said, "My partner is at the hotel, and I know she's going to have questions."

She looked at me, and her eyes filled with tears. "I thought I was over you." Then she got out of the car.

When I got to the hotel, all the lights were off, but I knew Joan was awake. I went directly to the shower without saying anything. When I got out, the lights were on. I knew I had some explaining to do, but I didn't know what or how to say what had happened. I knew Joan would blame it on her weight and lack of work. But I knew deep down it had nothing to do with her and everything to do with the fact that Shanae and I had unresolved issues we needed to work through. When I walked out of the bathroom, Joan just looked at me, her face full of sadness. She turned the lights back off. I got in bed and fell asleep. Joan never asked me one question.

11

FINDING A WAY OUT

By now, Joan's behavior had grown even more erratic, and it was starting to scare me. She had gained more than fifty pounds, and she was barely working. She started to drink more, and that was a sign to me that things had gotten worse. I didn't want to find myself in a relationship with someone like my mother. Joan was different, because she was never loud; instead, she hardly made a sound.

It was obvious that Joan and I had grown apart—or at least, I had grown apart from her. I wasn't happy, but I feared what would happen to her if we separated. She had no place to go. I couldn't image putting her in a situation where she was homeless. I didn't know what to do or say anymore. I wanted things to work, but the truth was that I was no longer attracted to Joan. Her weakness and lack of effort in her career were a complete turnoff, and her weight gain didn't help. Joan often did not do her hair or get dressed. I started to feel trapped in my own home. If not for my business trips, I would have gone insane.

One day, I came home from a work trip, and the condo was completely dark. There were curtains and towels hanging over every window, blocking the sunlight. I knew something was wrong, but I was afraid to find out what. I called for Joan, but there was no answer. I went to our bedroom, but she wasn't there. I started to panic and searched everywhere. She was nowhere to be found. I went to the kitchen to check for a note and found her under the kitchen table, staring at me. She frightened me. I had never seen her that way before. She just sat there in a daze. She looked as if she was possessed. I asked if she was OK, but she didn't respond. I asked if I could sit with her but was again met with silence. I made the decision to sit and asked how long she'd been down here. She turned away from me. I put my hand on her head and asked her when she'd last eaten. The kitchen looked the same as it had when I'd left home three days ago. She still didn't respond. I got up and prepared her some food. She stayed under the table the entire time I was cooking. I was nervous and felt I should call an ambulance, but I didn't want to startle her. I could tell something was going on mentally, but I didn't know what. I sat back down with her, bringing the soup I had made. This time, I sat in front of her, not giving her any room to move away from me. I told her she needed to eat and drink. Her lips were chapped from dehydration. I put some of the soup on a spoon and tried to feed her. She slowly opened her mouth. She took in the soup and started to cry. I immediately put my arms around her and told her it would be OK. I asked her to get up and sit at the table, and she did. I continued to feed her until she was done eating. We didn't talk, but tears were streaming down her face the entire time she ate. Before I knew it, I was crying too. I knew I had to get her help; my unhappiness didn't matter, because she needed me. After she was done eating, I got her to the shower and then into bed. I got in bed fully clothed and stayed with her until she fell asleep. I wasn't sure if she had been sleeping while I was gone, but I did know she hadn't had anything to eat or drink.

By the time Joan woke up, I had already looked up the names and numbers of a few therapists. I knew she needed to see someone, and I couldn't help her. It was obvious that she was too far gone. I was curious to know when this had started, but I didn't want to question her. I sat beside her and told her we needed to get her some help. She looked at me and nodded. I gave her the list of therapists I had compiled, but she asked me to pick a doctor for her and assured me she would go. After carefully looking over the list, I found one named Dr. Lee, who I thought was the best choice. I called to make an appointment for Joan. I told Dr. Lee about Joan's behavior, and she asked me to bring Joan in that day. I went to tell Joan that we were going to the doctor, but she wasn't on the bed. I called for her, but there was no response.

I found her on the bathroom floor, bleeding. There was blood everywhere. Joan had cut her wrists and was bleeding out. I wrapped a towel around her arms and then called an ambulance. The paramedics arrived within ten minutes. Joan was unconscious from blood loss and had no idea what was going on. I got in the ambulance with her and told the driver I was her partner. He nodded, and we left for the ER. When we arrived, there were patients everywhere, but Joan was seen immediately due to the nature of her injuries and her mental state.

I called Joan's mother, who lived in Austin, Texas. I told her about Joan's condition, but she seemed unbothered. I asked if she could come to New York to spend time with Joan, informing her that Joan had been diagnosed with bipolar disorder. She told me she couldn't but to call her when Joan got home. I felt sad for Joan. There was no way I was going to tell her I had called her mom and she'd said she wasn't coming. Joan was an only child, and her mother was her only family. There was no one else to call.

I took the week off to stay home with Joan. I didn't want to leave her alone. I knew all too well what that felt like. She got better each day with the medications she was taking and started talking and eating again. We talked more than we had in a while. The week went by quickly, and I felt OK to go back to work on Monday.

My feelings for Joan had neutralized, and I saw her as a friend. I was no longer attracted to her. Joan often tried to initiate sex or intimacy, but I had no desire. I had grown even unhappier in our relationship but didn't want her to have a setback by discussing it. Joan was often upset with me because I didn't want to have sex with her. I didn't have anyone I could really talk to, and I needed someone to listen.

One night, Joan and I went out with some friends, and everything was going well. A guy at the bar came to our table and offered to buy me a drink. I politely declined but thanked him with a smile. "Please take my number and call me," he said. I did and said good night. Joan immediately started to yell and scream. She was upset that I had taken his number. I was embarrassed. I told her I was just being nice and wasn't going to call him. I tried to calm Joan, but nothing was working. I left.

When I got home, I felt even more trapped by my situation. I felt like a kid locked in a room without a key. Joan had mood swings often, and it made it difficult for us to communicate. I waited for Joan to come home, but after a while, I fell asleep. I woke at two o'clock and realized Joan had not come in. I decided not to call her. When the phone rang, I thought it was her. It was Shanae. I was surprised. When I answered, she simply said hi. "Is everything OK? Is everyone OK?"

"Yes," she said, "everyone is OK. I was thinking of you, and I can't sleep, so I decided to call. You've been on my mind. Are you OK? How are you and Joan?"

I sighed. She asked again how Joan and I were doing. I was quiet at first but finally said, "Things aren't good, but I don't want to talk about it. How is your relationship?"

"Things are great, actually. I can't complain. I'm loved and happy, for the most part."

"That's great," I replied. "I'm happy to hear it."

There was an awkward silence, and then Shanae said, "She proposed to me."

I was silent, but my heart started to race, and my stomach started to do backflips. "Congratulations," I said.

"I said no," Shanae replied.

"Why?" I asked. "Did something happen?"

"No," she said. "I'm just not ready."

I was relieved but didn't know why. I told her being ready was important. We sat in silence awhile until we both fell asleep on the phone.

In the morning, I still had the phone to my ear, but the battery had died. I got out of bed, went to the kitchen, and saw that Joan was on the couch. I wasn't sure what time she had come in, but I knew it was after two o'clock. I fixed something to eat as quietly as I could, so as not to wake her. She came to the kitchen shortly thereafter to apologize. I was silent, because I really didn't want to talk about it. I could hear the frustration start to build in her voice because I wasn't responding, but I remained silent. I had prepared her a plate, and I sat down to eat, still without talking.

As I was eating, she asked, "Who were you talking to on the phone?"

I didn't respond.

She said, "Let me guess: Shanae." I stopped eating and left the table. She followed me to the room. "You two are in love. I'm not sure why you're with me and not her. Shanae would choose you over her partner." I allowed Joan to say all she needed to say. I had made up my mind that I wasn't going to respond, which was the best thing for both of us.

By now, all I was doing was working. I dreaded coming home. I slept on the couch most nights and showered in my guest bathroom most days. There was no intimacy at all between Joan and me at this point, and I was starting to grow lonely. We had been in this bad space for more than two years. I had contemplated going back to get my MBA, and the timing seem right. I wasn't distracted by a relationship, and I was settled at work. If I went to school full-time, then I could complete my MBA in two years. I enrolled at New York University.

A few months after I started school, things with Joan were still miserable. I finally told her we needed to talk. "I'm not happy, and I want to fully separate. I'll help you as much as I can, but I need my space and my home back. If we have any chance at being friends, then we need to separate."

Joan looked at me. "I'll get out. No problem."

I didn't want the conversation to go badly or for her to be upset. I knew I was asking for a lot, but I wanted peace more than ever. I was starting to feel like a trapped child again, and I had promised myself I would never allow that as an adult, because I had a choice. Joan started to pack her bags.

"Where will you go?" I asked. "You don't have to leave now."

Joan didn't respond. She made a phone call, and within an hour, someone came to help her move her things.

12

RUNNING THROUGH OPEN DOORS

Two years later, I felt at peace on graduation morning. After deciding to focus on myself and build a stronger relationship with God, I found myself more fulfilled. As I got dressed, I decided that today, doors would open. I had completed another chapter in my life, and I was ready to walk across the stage. Getting my MBA was solely for me. I didn't need it for my job or to advance in my career, but I needed it for me. My parents and a few friends were attending the ceremony.

I sat through many unknown names being called during the ceremony, and I saw many smiling faces and a few with tears. I heard my name, and I walked across the stage. I had received my MBA, and it was another item checked off my to-do list. I had worked very hard to complete my degree while working full-time. My focus now was to build on my newfound life. It felt normal to be single and alone. For the first time in a very long time, it was just me. I didn't depend on anyone and provided for myself. I had no baggage. I had no stress from others. I had no worries or lack of trust. I was enjoying some much-needed me time.

I was attending church and strengthening my relationship with God, and I had become more and more active with the youth in my community and church. I was in a clear state of mind, and giving back was my happy place. I enjoyed working with the kids at my church during my time off. Doors were opening, and I was finding my place without the expectations of a lover. My constant communication with God revealed many great things in my life, and I was in the midst of a breakthrough of some sort. I didn't know what that breakthrough was, but I knew the time was near.

I went once a month to visit my parents. My father was mentally and physically abusing my mother again, something I had seen often as a child. They were not in a healthy relationship, but it was good for us all to get together. My parents also came to New York every few months to visit me. I was building relationships with my mother and father individually. Things with my mother were still very rocky, but we were making progress. Although they were in a very unhealthy space, they both were trying to be better parents.

I was ready to travel more. I had given so much of myself to my job and to my relationships that I wasn't taking enough time for myself. I decided to go on a cruise with some friends. The cruise left from New York and went to several different parts of Mexico. I had heard about it from a friend, who had gone on it for the last five years. It was a party cruise: people had sex, danced, and got drunk. In other words, it was a fun ship where people left their worries behind. I was hoping it would be a new beginning.

Tim and Mona, two of my closest friends, were more like my siblings. For the first time, I felt as though I had a brother and sister. Tim was a strong, tall, and handsome man. He had the body of a comic-book action hero. Mona was also tall but thin. She was a beautiful woman inside and out. She attracted great people and energy all around her. We all vowed to have a great time and party, and we did just that.

By the second night of the cruise, Tim and Mona each had met a special someone. While some people showed interest in me, I didn't want my space invaded. I wasn't ready yet, or maybe I hadn't met the right person yet. It had been nearly two years since I'd had a relationship. I'd been single since Joan and hadn't had sex. I was waiting for the right person to find me, and I didn't want to ruin a wonderful vacation with my friends. I kept to myself and enjoyed the cruise.

On one of the excursions off the ship, we decided to go to one of the small local beaches for the day. We knew a few people on the cruise who were going to this particular beach, so we decided to join them. Tim and Mona are very outgoing and were constantly in the middle of everything. While they were all over the beach meeting new people, I stayed on my chair and enjoyed the sun. I heard them approach me, but I didn't open my eyes. They were both laughing like schoolchildren, so I finally looked up at them. With them was a handsome and well-built man. He had beautiful hair and a smile to die for. Tim said, "Sister, I want you to meet Richard." Before I could say hello, Richard extended his hand and introduced himself.

I smiled and said, "Nice to meet you, Richard. I'm Rachel."

"I've heard a lot of great things about you from your friends, and I've seen you a few times on the cruise."

I smiled. "I'm sorry; this is my first time seeing you."

He laughed. "It's OK. There's a lot to look at on this cruise."

"I guess I'm just unlucky, because I haven't seen much!" He smiled, and we began to talk.

Before we knew it, it was time to head back to the cruise ship. Before parting ways, Richard asked what room I was in and if he could come by so we could continue our conversation. I smiled and said no. He looked surprised. "If I find you on the cruise ship, will you talk to me?" I smiled and said yes. We parted ways, found our friends, and headed to the ship.

When we were back on the ship, Mona asked, "What did you and Richard talk about all that time?"

I smiled. "Stuff."

That piqued Tim's interest, and they both asked me question after question.

"He's a nice guy, but I'm not interested."

At the same time, they said, "You can't be single forever."

We were at dinner when I felt a warm hand on my shoulder. It was Richard. I was a bit surprised, as I hadn't thought I would see him again. He was all cleaned up and had on a tie. He was very handsome, and his smile was beautiful. He asked if he could sit with us. Before I could respond, Mona said yes. We all laughed and talked. Mona and Tim both were drinking. To my surprise, Richard did not drink much. He had a glass of wine but said he wasn't a heavy drinker.

Tim said, "You two have that in common, so I'll drink enough for both of you." We all laughed and carried on with dinner.

Richard and I talked all night as we watched the stars. The sky was open, and the stars were shining bright. Richard was very nice and smart. He also lived in New York. We discovered that we lived only fifteen minutes from each other. *It's a very small world*, I thought to myself. *You never know who your neighbor is.* Before I knew it, the sun was coming up. What an amazing sight to see the sunrise in the middle of the ocean on a cruise ship. We both watched in silence until I excused myself to get some sleep before the day's festivities. I had a lot planned with Mona and Tim, and I didn't want to be dragging. I decided to skip breakfast and sleep so I would be ready. Richard walked me to my cabin, and we said our goodbyes. As I closed the door, he said, "We should hang out when we get back home. I'm from New York, and I know all the hot spots."

I smiled. "Maybe."

On the last day of the cruise, we had a great day of festivities ahead of us. When we got off the cruise ship, we planned to shop all day long. When I met up with Tim and Mona, they asked me if I had stayed with Richard the night before. I said yes, but before I could explain, they both asked for the hot, nasty details. I said, "We watched the stars and talked outside until morning." They both looked perplexed, and I knew they were confused.

Mona asked, "So all you did was talk all night?"

I laughed. "Yes!"

Tim said, "That could not have been me."

Shopping was fun, but we were all tired from the long day of walking and shopping. We agreed to skip dinner and instead pack our things so we'd be ready to disembark from the ship the next morning. I was exhausted when I got to my cabin. I had a few messages from Richard, but I didn't return them. I didn't want to give him the wrong impression, so I decided I would end things there. I packed my things and showered. I was exhausted and went to bed. The next morning, I went out to my balcony for one last view of the ocean. It was an amazing sight and very peaceful, but it was time to head back to the real world.

We all met for breakfast and agreed to take a yearly trip together. We'd had so much fun, and we didn't want it to end in Mexico. We sat at the breakfast table until it was time to leave. When our group was called, we happily got off the ship to get our bags. We called an Uber and chatted as we waited. Everyone had parked at my house, because my place was close to the port. We rode home in silence. We were all tired. When we arrived, we said goodbye, and Mona and Tim went straight to their cars.

When I went inside, I dropped my bags at the door and found my bed. I was happy to sleep in my California king bed. The cruise was awesome, but my bed on the ship did not compare to my bed at home. I grabbed my laptop and logged in to my Facebook account. Richard had found me on social media and had invited me to a dinner at his home. He had a dinner each year and invited his friends. He also mentioned going to a local club to dance. I smiled. I couldn't believe he had found me so quickly. I felt bad, because I hadn't returned his last few messages on the cruise ship, and we hadn't exchanged information while on the ship. He wanted to show me the city, so I responded and gave him my number. I told him I would attend his dinner party.

13

NO TURNING BACK

Richard and I had become great friends. We spent a lot of time together when I wasn't away for work. We had a lot in common, yet we were so very different. We still talked all night when time permitted. One night, as we were walking into a dinner party at Richard's friend's house, Richard said, "I love you, and you're going to be my wife."

I looked at him. "I don't want to be married, and I don't want a relationship." Richard and I had not had sex; we hadn't even kissed. We were just friends. I didn't want to ruin that, and I felt that could happen if we tried to date.

"I know you're not ready, and that's OK," he said. "I'm going to wait."

The party was fun, but I was distracted the entire night thinking about what Richard had said. I was worried that our friendship was coming to an end. When we got back my place, I asked him if he was upset with me. He smiled. "No. I'm not talking because you seem to be thinking."

"Yes, I suppose I am," I said.

He laughed. "I know."

We sat in silence. Finally, I said, "My relationships don't work out. I'm bad with love and trust. I don't trust people, and I don't like feeling trapped." I told him about my childhood and my parents, so he would better understand my issues. I told him about my granny. He listened and took it all in without a word.

When I was done, he said, "I love you, and I will wait on you. I will move at your pace, and I will wait. No matter what, you're stuck with me forever. Promise me that we will always be friends."

I looked at him. "I promise."

Months passed, and Richard and I were still just friends, but I could feel things changing. I was starting to fall for him, and I knew it. He often told me he loved me, but he never pressured me to say it back. By now, we were like high school kids on the phone all night. We e-mailed each other throughout the day. We were together every moment we weren't working. Richard didn't travel for work, so his schedule was much more flexible. He worked for the government as an IT specialist, and before that, he had been in the navy for eight years.

My birthday was approaching, and I decided I would invite Richard to celebrate with me. I planned to go to Italy. Neither of us had ever been, and I thought it would be fun. He loved to plan things and was very excited when I asked him. I was turning twenty-eight, and I wanted to travel. We planned a seven-day trip to Venice and Milan that would be filled with history, good food, shopping, and sightseeing.

We arrived at the Hotel Londra Palace in Venice. The suite was beautiful, and the view was breathtaking. The hotel had only fifty-three rooms. Our room faced the Venetian Lagoon, and the view of the water was very calming. I could have spent the entire vacation in that room. I decided to shower, dress, and head out on the town. I was very excited, and there was much to see. Richard was also excited and ready to tour the town. We had plans for a dinner cruise, and it was the perfect idea for our first night. The water was relaxing. Dinner was delightful, and we had great conversation. It felt perfect. My life felt perfect in that moment. After dinner, we danced on the boat, along with the other couples. It was a happy place and one without worry, if only for that time.

We were exhausted when we arrived at the hotel. We prepared for bed and were both sound asleep before we knew it. We slept peacefully as one. Richard had the next day planned, and we were ready to tackle Venice. We toured several museums. We took in and learned about the culture, one that was very different from our own. Things were much slower. No one was in a rush. It was pleasantly smooth, and everyone seemed to be without worry. In the United States, we are born into worry—at least, that was my story. We enjoyed a beautiful day and evening. We decided to make it an early night, because we were heading to Milan in the morning.

We stood at the balcony of our room, talking and learning more about each other. We told each other the stories of who we were and how we had gotten to the very point where we were. We connected differently, and we both could feel it. The feeling did not require words. For the first time, I felt that my future was in front of me—my future was with Richard. As we continued to talk, Richard held me close and often kissed my lips. He gently touched my face and ran his fingers through my hair. In a moment of silence, he looked into my eyes and said, "I love you, and you will marry me one day." I was without words, but I felt that he was right.

We made love for the first time that night, and we enjoyed the essence of each other. With every touch and kiss, I felt chills, yet my body was warm. The connection of our bodies felt whole. I felt complete. I felt safe. I felt loved. And then my heart felt as if it had stopped. I realized I was afraid—afraid to fall, afraid he wouldn't catch me. In the midst of that thought, I felt my body grow into an orgasm. My body shivered, and my heart raced. His orgasm followed, and we lay silently together. The silence turned into sleep.

Milan was all that I had imagined: shops and boutiques everywhere. I was in heaven, and I could tell

Richard got a kick out of seeing me so happy. I loved to shop; it was one of my favorite pastimes. Richard didn't share my passion for shopping, but he was easy to please, and as long as we were together, he was happy. There was mist in the air and fog as far as we could see. The scenery was simply amazing. There were a lot of people on bikes and on foot. There were lots of shopping bags in hands and much chatter among the shoppers. I fell in love with several stores. I was in shopping heaven, and I loved it.

We toured Venice and Milan, and it was a great adventure. We had enjoyed our stay, but it was time to head back to our world. Although it was bittersweet to leave, it was time to get back to reality. Our flight was on time, and the plane was filled. We stayed up the entire flight talking and laughing, while everyone around us slept. I could tell Richard didn't want the trip to end, but we both knew it was time.

Back home, we settled into our normal routines. We grew closer with each passing day. Things were starting to feel permanent without the conversation about commitment. We spent all our free time together. On one occasion, we both worked a long day, and we were eager to lie on the couch and watch a movie. We had dinner, and I told Richard I was going to shower before the movie. It was a Friday night, so neither of us was concerned with time. When I got out of the shower, I saw Richard looking at his phone. He seemed upset, but I didn't ask. As I dressed, I heard his phone ring, but he didn't answer. Then it rang again. I finally asked if everything was OK. He said yes and turned his phone off. This was the night his ex-girlfriend Dana showed up at my place.

I was upset. Richard told me that, although he and Dana lived together, he was single and had been for some time. From the looks of this woman, she was very much in a relationship with him, even if he wasn't with her. I felt pieces of my soul starting to break. I had trusted and believed him. We had spent so much time together that I never suspected another woman to be knocking on my door. Instead of going to the couch, I locked my door and went to bed confused. I wanted to know who she was. I wanted an explanation, but I didn't want to see his face.

The next day, Richard called many times until finally, I blocked his number. He came to my place and e-mailed me as well. I didn't respond to anything. I was hurt and felt betrayed. I didn't know what to do or think. I knew I needed to get out of my place and get some fresh air. When I opened the door, Dana was standing there, waiting on me. I didn't know what to think other than that I was going to defend myself, because I was sure she was there for trouble.

She looked at me with sad eyes and said, "I can see why he wants you." I stood in silence. I could tell she had been drinking and was perhaps even high. "He's been with you all this time, and I thought he was working. Did he tell you about me? Did he tell you we were together for ten years? Did he tell you anything about me?"

I looked at her and felt sad, because she was clearly hurting. I finally said, "No, he never mentioned you in detail, only that you were his ex." We stood there in silence for a moment.

As I was about to speak, I saw Richard approach us. He looked like he hadn't slept. In an aggressive but soft voice, he said, "Dana, leave her out of this. She has nothing to do with this." I was even more confused. He was talking to her like she had a mental disorder.

She looked at him and asked, "Do you love her? Is she who you want to be with?"

He looked at me and then at Dana and said, "Yes, I love her, and one day, I hope she becomes my wife." I was even more confused.

She said to him now, yelling and crying, "What about us? What about me?"

Richard walked closer to her and said, "We're over, and we have been over. I wasn't happy, and now I am. Come with me. Let me take you home." He looked back at me and whispered, "I'm sorry," and then walked away. I was completely lost and confused but realized there was more to this story that I needed to know. I unblocked Richard and sent him a text, asking him to call me when he was free. He responded instantly and said he would.

14

LONG TIME COMING

Richard and I were back to our normal happy lives. We decided we didn't want to live apart any longer, so Richard moved into my place. I was happy again, but this time was a little different from before. I wasn't sure what it was, but it was different. Richard had been talking about children and marriage a lot. Before Richard, I hadn't wanted children, but being with him had changed my mind; however, the thought of marriage scared me to death. I had never wanted to be married. I hadn't been a little girl who dreamed about wedding dresses.

We were both working a lot of hours, and we wanted to take a vacation and get away. We decided we would go somewhere warm with a beach and booked a flight to Aruba for a few days. The vacation was planned at the last minute, so I didn't have time to do anything or to tell anyone we were leaving. All I had time to do was request the time off from my job. Work was a piece of cake, as I made my own schedule. By this time, I had become president of public relations and marketing.

We checked into our room at the Renaissance by Marriott. In the natural flow of vacation, we got dressed and headed out on the town. We found food and shops. We walked and talked until we were tired. When we got back to our room, Richard took a shower, and I went outside, as our room faced the ocean. Directly in front of our room was a beautiful white pavilion with a bench swing. I sat on the swing and watched the water. There was something very calming about the ocean. It was a place where creatures lived, and that gave humans like me peace.

Richard sat beside me, and we talked and laughed. There was a different energy between us that was often filled with long periods of silence. I looked away from the water and into his eyes. For the first time, I said, "I love you too." He smiled so big he could have taken the entire ocean in. I smiled too and looked back to the ocean.

When I turned back to him, he was on one knee. He looked into my eyes and said, "I want to spend the rest of my life with you. Will you marry me?" I smiled and said yes. The ring was simply beautiful: a five-carat diamond on a platinum band. The ring screamed, "You can't say no to this!" That night was the beginning of my forever.

We returned home to our condo as an engaged couple. It all hit me at once. I was engaged. I needed to call Mona and Tim. I needed to call my parents. I knew there would be a lot of questions. I knew when I returned to work with a five-carat diamond on my finger, I would be stopped by everyone who saw me. It all had happened so fast. Richard and I had dated for only eighteen months, and we were already engaged. We spent the night in as we prepared for work the next day. Before we turned the lights out, he asked, "Are you ready for tomorrow?"

"I've never been more ready," I said. I knew he was asking if I was ready to tell the world I would soon be his bride.

On my way into my office, I called my mom and dad. They were both very excited and said they would visit that weekend. Next, I called Mona. She was very surprised and sounded as if she wasn't happy for me. I could hear it in her voice and felt that something was bothering her. I decided not to ask. I then called Tim, and he was very excited; an eavesdropper would have thought *he* was the one getting married. I told Tim about Mona's reaction to my engagement, and he said, "I'm not surprised; I think she is in love with you." I was puzzled and thought this was something Mona should have spoken to me about.

I told all the important people in my life, and now it was time to answer all the questions from the people in my office. Everything went well. Everyone came to my office at some point throughout the day as they heard the good news from another associate.

When I arrived home, Richard asked me how my day had gone and how often I'd had to repeat myself. We looked at each other and laughed. He could imagine without my saying a word that I had spent my entire day talking about my ring and him. I asked him about his day and if he had spoken with his parents. He said, "My parents knew before I proposed. I didn't have anyone to call. The people closest to me knew I was ring shopping six months ago. It took me a long time to find the perfect ring."

"You knew you wanted to get married six months ago?" I asked.

Richard looked at me. "No. I knew I wanted to marry you eighteen months ago. I was just waiting for you to be ready."

We had been engaged for a few months and were in the process of planning the wedding and rehearsal dinner with our families and friends. We decided to do a destination wedding. We would get married in Paris with a guest list of thirty.

I had not thought to call or tell Shanae that I was engaged. I had actually not thought about her at all for the last eighteen months. In the midst of planning my engagement dinner in Georgia, she came into my mind, as she was a part of my past. I also realized I'd never told Richard about Shanae, although I had told him about all my other relationships. I picked up the phone and dialed her number. She answered on the third ring. I had not heard her voice in a long time, and it made me nervous when she answered. I said, "Hi, stranger. How are you? How's life?"

In a calm but stern voice she responded, "I'm good. And you?" I said the same, and we proceeded to catch up on our lives. We hadn't talked in such a long time that I couldn't remember when we'd last spoken. I did know I hadn't talked to her since Richard had come into my life.

Eventually, I said, "I'm calling to tell you I'm getting married."

There was a silence, and then she said, "Congratulations. I'm happy for you."

"I'd love for you to attend my engagement dinner in Georgia." Shanae hesitated but then said she'd be there. I was happy to know she would be. I realized we needed to be friends; we shared too much to not speak to each other.

The engagement dinner was wonderful. Everyone was there, including my coach; my high school friends; and, of course, my family. However, there was one person missing: my father. He had stayed out the night before using drugs, and I knew he wasn't going to be there to support me. I was sad, but I refused to let anything get in the way of that day. It was strange to see Shanae at my engagement dinner. I could tell she worked out often. She was still beautiful to me. We had shared so much, and we had grown so far apart. She was very quiet. If I hadn't physically seen her, then I would not have known she was there.

Shanae and I agreed to remain friends and to stay in touch. Shanae had been with the same partner for years at this point, and from what I could see, she was happy. I was happy for her and happy for us. We had both found love, and we were both living happy lives. Richard and I said goodbye to our guests and headed to the hotel. We were flying back to New York the following day.

Wedding planning was crazy and stressful at times. Finding a dress and communicating with our wedding planner was a task. I was thankful to have such a great wedding planner. Mona and I had not been talking much at all. She kept her distance, so I knew she was bothered that I was getting married. Shanae and I talked a few times a week, and she was very supportive as I got ready for my big day. My mom was excited and ready to be in my wedding. Tim was a great help and constantly made sure I was OK. Richard was amazing as he assisted with the entire planning process. Even though it was very stressful, everything fell into place.

At the wedding rehearsal, the facility was just beautiful. Our wedding planner was fantastic, and she had captured my vision perfectly. The flowers were all handpicked white roses. The ballroom was completely white with a high ceiling. The rehearsal went smoothly, and everyone was ready. Instead of having separate bachelor and bachelorette parties, we decided to take our guests to Moulin Rouge. We had a great time and were all anxious for the next day, the wedding.

It was a perfect morning. The photographer was early and ready to capture the day. My wedding party was set and in place. My hairstylist and makeup artist were on time. It was a perfect morning for me to become Mrs. Rachel Reynolds-Tull. I could hear the music and knew everyone was in place. I saw tears falling from my mother's eyes, and for a moment, I felt a sadness, because my granny and father wasn't there. It was a short-lived moment.

My mother and I embraced, the doors opened, and my song played—"A Couple of Forevers" by Chrisette Michele. It looked like heaven. There were thousands of white roses, the room was completely white, all our guests had on black and white, and there were crystals hanging from above. It was heaven on earth. I looked down the aisle and saw Richard standing tall. He was the most handsome man I had ever seen. As the tears fell from his eyes and I got closer to him, I could feel his heart and see his truth. He loved me, and he was there to protect me. He was my white knight. We said our vows and made the ultimate promise to God in front of our families and friends. We were now one. When I looked at our guests, there wasn't a dry eye.

We walked down a flight of stairs covered in red carpet. Horns played for us. Two large french doors made for kings and queens opened, and we walked out into the sunlight, where our car waited. We drove to the Eiffel Tower for our wedding photos. It was a bright sunny day. Afterward, we went to the court-yard for more photos before dining with our families and friends. The day had gone by quickly, but the night was still young. At the reception, we danced the night away. Richard and I laughed and enjoyed each other. When the night came to an end, we found our-selves still full of energy. For the first time, we made love until the sun came up as Mr. and Mrs. Tull.

We honeymooned for twelve days and visited five countries: England, Spain, Portugal, the Czech Republic, and France. We stayed in Barcelona on the Mediterranean Sea. Our hotel was beyond our imagi-nations, and we spent a lot of time on the beach. We enjoyed every single day of our honeymoon as if it were our last. We took in the culture of each country, and we came away with something from each that made our honeymoon even more special. It was a time never to forget. It was magical.

15

LOVE CONQUERS ALL

We were married and fully becoming one unit. Our work lives were busier than ever, and we were focused on building our family, careers, and marriage. We still had a lot of fun together and were happy to celebrate our first year of marriage. We were stronger than ever and prepared to take on the world. Although work was good for me, I was ready to do something different and to branch out. I wanted to become an entrepreneur. Richard was very supportive and pushed me to do just that, but I was afraid. I was unsure if I would be successful. Failure was a scary thing to me. I had very high expectations of myself.

Richard and I had started to talk about having kids. I wasn't sure if I was ready, but I had promised him I would have his children, and he was eager to become a father. I wasn't sure if I could start my own business with a newborn or even manage motherhood with my current workload. But with Richard by my side, I felt I could do anything, so I agreed to have a child.

As days and months passed, we were patient. I had grown to want a child as much as Richard did, and I began to love the thought of being a mother, of being something to a child that I'd never had myself. I was ready. Summer was approaching, and I had not yet conceived, so Richard and I decided to follow up with my doctors. They reassured us that I was perfectly healthy. I had feared that I couldn't have children. We were both relieved.

One Sunday, I realized my cycle was late, which could mean that what we were wishing for was near. I told Richard, and we both dashed to the door. We went to the local drugstore for a pregnancy test. When we arrived back at the condo, I immediately went to the bathroom to take the test. Richard was right on my heels. I took the test, and we waited. We were anxious and hopeful at the same time. I had a feeling of excitement despite the nervousness. Finally, it was time to look at the stick, but I couldn't, so I asked Richard to do it. There was silence, which scared me. I had started to feel like I had failed. Then, Richard yelled that we were going to have a baby. It was music to my ears, and we both danced in the bathroom, enjoying this moment as we realized our newest family member was growing in my belly.

Pregnancy was great. I enjoyed caring for our son, and Richard was in love with the fact that we were having a boy. Richard became very protective during my pregnancy, and we both were particular about the things we did. As the delivery date approached, we focused on having a healthy baby.

Finally, the time had come. Our son was ready to enter the world. My water broke, and we prepared to go to the hospital. When we arrived, my doctor was already there. I was happy and ready to deliver. By now, I was larger than I cared to be, and I was more and more uncomfortable. I was in labor for twelve hours, and in the last seconds of my son's birth, I knew I had a greater purpose in life: to become a mother.

I heard a soft scream, and he was here. Our baby boy was born. We named him Richard Reynolds Tull. Several emotions hit me all at once, and when I saw his face, all the love I had inside me poured directly into him. I was a mother and a protector of God's creation. My life had changed forever.

AUTHOR BIOGRAPHY

 Raquel M. R. Thomas is a writer and business owner from Columbia, South Carolina. A mother of two children, she believes in the value of education and hard work and strives to demonstrate those values to young people. What Becomes of a Broken Soul is based on events in Raquel's life and displays her drive to achieve her dreams.

Raquel is using her success and achievements to help those just like her; those who may not have the support or recourses, but possess the drive and vision to see beyond their circumstances. Raquel believed even as a child that she could bring her youthful musings to life; her life! The debut of her first fictional book is the realization of an early desire to become a writer, and now the writings of a troubled 2nd grader will inspire and motivate the masses.

64820695R00115

Made in the USA
Lexington, KY
21 June 2017